MW01144655

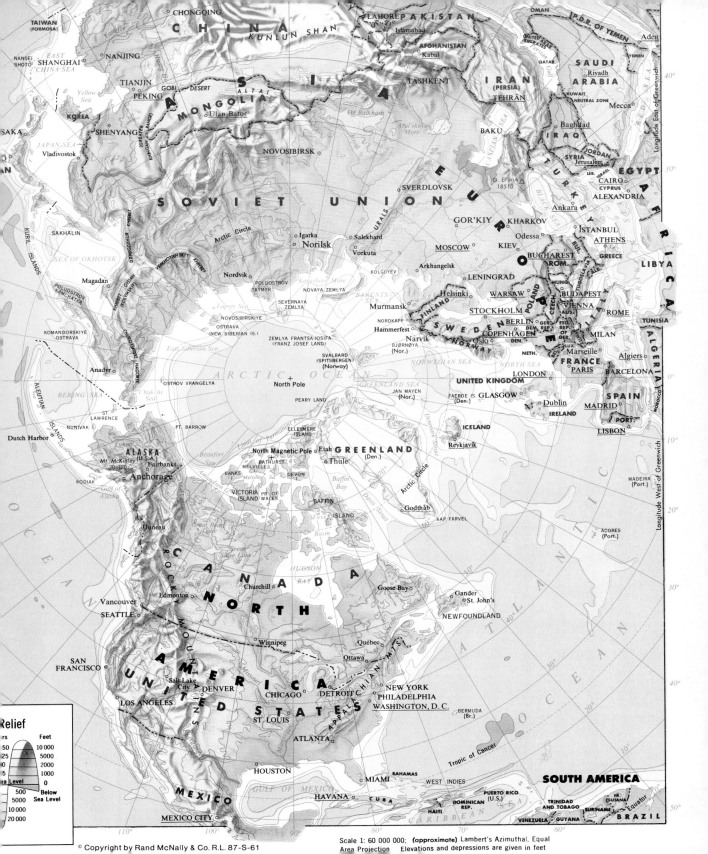

TAIWAN
(FORMOSA)
NANSEI
SHOTO
EAST
CHINA SEA
SHANGHAI
Yellow
Sea
KOREA
OSAKA
JAPAN SEA
Vladivostok

CHONGQING
CHINA
KUNLUN SHAN
Yangtze
NANJING
TIANJIN
PEKING
GOBI DESERT
ALTAI
SHENYANG
Ulan Bator
MONGOLIA
ASIA
NOVOSIBIRSK
KHINGAN RANGE
GREATER
SAKHALIN
SEA OF OKHOTSK
Magadan
POLUOSTROV
KAMCHATKA
KOMANDORSKIYE
OSTRAVA
Anadyr
DZHUGDZHUR
KHREBET CYDAN
KOLYASKIY
CHUKOTSKIY NAGORIYE
OSTROV VRANGELYA
Chukchi
Sea

SOVIET UNION
Oz. Balkhash
Aral'skoye
More
Arctic Circle
Igarka
Norilsk
Salekhard
Vorkuta
Yenisey
Ob'
VERKHOYANSKIY KHREBET
Nordvik
POLUOSTROV TAYMYR
Karskoye More
NOVOSIBIRSKIYE OSTRAVA
(NEW SIBERIAN IS.)
ZEMLYA FRANTSA-IOSIFA
(FRANZ JOSEF LAND)
Laptev Sea
SEVERNAYA
ZEMLYA
NOVAYA ZEMLYA
East Siberian Sea
ARCTIC OCEAN
North Pole

LAHORE PAKISTAN
Islamabad
AFGHANISTAN
Kabul
TASHKENT
IRAN
(PERSIA)
TEHRĀN
SVERDLOVSK
URALS
BAKU
CASPIAN SEA
EUROPE
GOR'KIY KHARKOV
MOSCOW KIEV
Arkhangelsk
LENINGRAD
KOLGUYEV
Helsinki
WARSAW
STOCKHOLM
BARENTS SEA
Murmansk
NORDKAPP
Hammerfest
Narvik
BJØRNØYA
(Nor.)
SVALBARD
(SPITSBERGEN)
(Norway)
JAN MAYEN
(Nor.)
FINLAND
SWEDEN
NORWAY
Oslo
BERLIN
COPENHAGEN
DEN.
NETH.
NORWEGIAN SEA
NORTH SEA
UNITED KINGDOM
LONDON
FAEROE IS GLASGOW
(Den.)
Dublin
IRELAND

OMAN
P.D.R. OF YEMEN
Aden
UNITED ARAB EMIRATES
QATAR
YEMEN
SAUDI ARABIA
Riyadh
KUWAIT
NEUTRAL ZONE
Mecca
RED SEA
Baghdad
IRAQ
JORDAN
SYRIA
Jerusalem
TURKEY
ISTANBUL
Ankara
ATHENS
GREECE
BUCHAREST
ROM.
HUNG.
BUDAPEST
VIENNA
AUS.
ROME
MILAN
YUGOSLAVIA
POLAND
CZECH.
GER.
DEM. REP.
FED. REP. OF GER.
LUX.
FRANCE
PARIS
Marseille
Algiers
BARCELONA
SPAIN
MADRID
PORT.
LISBON
Longitude East of Greenwich
EGYPT
CAIRO
CYPRUS
ALEXANDRIA
AFRICA
LIBYA
TUNISIA
ALGERIA
MOROCCO
MADEIRA
(Port.)
30°
20°
G. El'brus
18510
BLACK SEA

ICELAND
Reykjavík
ACORES
(Port.)
ATLANTIC
GREENLAND
(Den.)
Thule
Etah
Godthåb
KAP FARVEL
GREENLAND SEA
Peary Land
ELLESMERE ISLAND
North Magnetic Pole
BATHURST
MELVILLE
DEVON
BANKS
VICTORIA
ISLAND
PR. OF WALES
BAFFIN
ISLAND
Baffin
Bay
Davis Strait
ALASKA
(U.S.A.)
Mt. McKinley
20.320
Fairbanks
Anchorage
KODIAK
ST LAWRENCE
NUNIVAK
Dutch Harbor
BERING SEA
ALEUTIAN ISLANDS
PT. BARROW
Beaufort
Sea
Amundsen Gulf
Great Bear
Lake
Great
Slave Lake
CANADA
ROCKY MOUNTAINS
Juneau
Vancouver
SEATTLE
SAN FRANCISCO
LOS ANGELES
Salt Lake City
DENVER
Edmonton
Churchill
HUDSON BAY
Winnipeg
NORTH
AMERICA
UNITED STATES
CHICAGO
ST. LOUIS
ATLANTA
DETROIT
MISSOURI
APPALACHIAN MTS.
Québec
Ottawa
NEW YORK
PHILADELPHIA
WASHINGTON, D.C.
Goose Bay
Gander
St. John's
NEWFOUNDLAND
BERMUDA
(Br.)
OCEAN
Arctic Circle
HOUSTON
MEXICO
MEXICO CITY
GULF OF MEXICO
MIAMI
HAVANA
CUBA
BAHAMAS
WEST INDIES
HAITI
DOMINICAN REP.
PUERTO RICO
(U.S.)
CARIBBEAN
TRINIDAD AND TOBAGO
VENEZUELA
GUYANA
SURINAME
FR. GUIANA
BRAZIL
SOUTH AMERICA
Equator
Tropic of Cancer
PACIFIC OCEAN
50°
40°
30°
20°
10°

Longitude West of Greenwich

Relief

ers	Feet
50	10 000
25	5000
0	2000
5	1000
Sea Level	0
	Below Sea Level
500	
5000	
1 000	
20 000	

© Copyright by Rand McNally & Co. R.L. 87-S-61

Scale 1: 60 000 000; (approximate) Lambert's Azimuthal, Equal Area Projection   Elevations and depressions are given in feet

Enchantment of the World

CANADA

By Jenifer Shepherd

Consultant: Carman Miller, Ph.D., Department of History, McGill University, Montreal, Canada

Consultant for Reading: Robert L. Hillerich, Ph.D., Bowling Green State University, Bowling Green, Ohio

CHILDRENS PRESS ®

CHICAGO

Ethnic celebrations are popular in Canada.

Library of Congress Cataloging-in-Publication Data
Shepherd, Jenifer A.
  Canada.
  (Enchantment of the world)
  Includes index.
  Summary: Introduces our northern neighbor, its history
and geography, government, people, and culture.
  1. Canada—Juvenile literature. [1. Canada]
I. Title. II. Series.
F1008.2.S48 1987   971   87-14626
ISBN 0-516-02757-3

Childrens Press®, Chicago
Copyright © 1987 by Regensteiner Publishing Enterprises, Inc.
All rights reserved. Published simultaneously in Canada.
Printed in the United States of America.
    8 9 10 R 01 00 99 98 97 96

Picture Acknowledgments
Cameramann International, Ltd.: Pages 4 (left), 6
(2 photos), 11 (right), 31 (left), 65, 67 (2 photos), 71, 72
(right), 73, 75 (right), 76 (left), 84 (center right and
bottom), 87 (top), 88 (top left), 89, 96, 97 (2 photos), 112,
122 (2 photos), 124 (left).
© **W. Ray Scott:** Pages 4 (right), 53 (left)
Third Coast: © Betsy Fernald-Maier, Page 5; © Jack Kurtz,
Page 99 (top left).
Tom Stack & Associates: © Sharon Gerig, Page 8; © Gary
Milburn, Pages 21 (right), 127 (bottom); © Thomas
Kitchin, Pages 32, 44 (left), 72 (left), 79 (bottom
right), 117 (bottom right); © Steve Elmore, Page 79 (right);
© Stephen Peterson, Page 127 (top).
H. Armstrong Roberts: Pages 9 (left), 38 (left), 39, 46, 48,
51 (right), 53 (right); © M. Spector, Page 18 (right);
© George Hunter, Pages 19, 83, 101; © L. Burton, Page 22;
© P. Degginger, Page 51 (left); © Ralph Krubner, Page 103
(right); © Merrithew/Miller, Page 62; © W. Clark, Page 139;
© Damm/Zefa, Pages 87 (center), 110 (bottom left).
Valan Photos: © Harold V. Green, Pages 9 (right), 80
(bottom), 82; © Carl Bigras, Cover, Pages 12 (top), 64, 93;
© Wayne Lankinen, Page 16; © Ken Patterson, Page 21 (top
left); © Wayne Shield, Page 21 (bottom left); © Thomas
Kitchin, Pages 23, 26 (top), 68 (bottom), 92 (left); © Denis
Roy, Pages 25 (top left), 108 (left), 115 (top); © J. R. Page,
Pages 25 (bottom left), 34, 115 (bottom); © John Fowler,
Pages 25 (top right), 68 (top left), 94 (left); © Jean-Marie
Jro, Page 26 (bottom center); © Frank E. Johnson, Page 31
(right); © Karen D. Rooney, Pages 36 (right), 98 (right);
© O.J. Hugessen, Page 38 (right); © Tom W. Parkin, Page
45; © Michael J. Johnson, Pages 55, 74 (top left); © Martin
Kuhnigk, Pages 68 (top right), 88 (bottom); © Irwin
Barrett, Page 74 (top right); © V. Wilkinson, Page 74
(bottom); © V. Whelan, Pages 75 (left), 99 (bottom right);
© Pierre Kohler, Page 84 (top); © Kennon Cooke, Pages 87
(bottom), 95 (bottom), 102 (bottom right), 107, 117 (top),
119, 124 (left); © Joseph R. Pearce, Page 95 (top); © J.A.
Wilkinson, Page 103 (left); © Stephen Krasemann, Pages
108 (right), 109 (left); © Pam Hickman, Page 109 (right);
© Francis Lepine, Page 116.
Marilyn Gartman Agency: © Michael Philip Manheim,
Pages 11 (left), 84 (center left), 90, 91 (bottom left), 102
(bottom left), 110 (top).
Nawrocki Stock Photo: © Wm. S. Nawrocki, Pages 26
(bottom right and left), 58 (top), 66, 94 (right), 102 (top);
© Jeff Apoian, Page 12 (bottom); © Robert Perron, Page 99
(bottom left).
Odyssey Productions: © Robert Frerck, Pages 17
(2 photos), 18 (left), 85 (left), 88 (top right), 104 (right),
105, 106.
Root Resources: © Kenneth W. Fink, Pages 25 (bottom
right), 110 (bottom right); © J. Downton, Page 44 (right);
© Evelyn Davidson, Page 104 (left); © Larry Schaefer, Page
117 (bottom left); © Byron Crader, Page 118.
© **Reinhard Brucker:** Pages 36 (left), 43.
Historical Pictures Service, Inc., Chicago: Page 50.
United Press International: Page 57.
The Photo Source: Pages 58 (center), 91 (top), 98 (left).
Department of Regional Industrial Expansion, Canada:
Pages 76 (right), 100.
© **Chandler Forman:** Pages 77, 125.
© **Joan Dunlop:** Page 80 (top).
Image Finders: © A. Osinski, Page 85 (right).
EKM-Nepenthe: © Kurt Thorson, Page 92 (right); © James
F. Pribble, Pages 99 (top right), 120; © Klaus Werner, Page 113.
© **Virginia Grimes:** Page 124 (bottom right).
Roloc Color Slides: Cover (inset).
Len W. Meents: Maps on pages 12, 15, 82.
**Courtesy Flag Research Center, Winchester,
Massachusetts 01980:** Flag on back cover.
Cover: Parliament building, Ottawa; Bow River, Alberta (inset).

Butchart Gardens near Victoria, British Columbia

TABLE OF CONTENTS

People from all parts of the world now live in Toronto and they retain much of their individual culture.

Chapter 1

A LAND OF IMMIGRANTS

For ten days each June in Toronto, Ontario, the community
centers and church halls of the many different ethnic groups open
their doors to the people of the city in a festival called Caravan.
Visitors buy passports that allow them to go to as many pavilions
as they wish. They can learn such things as *ikebana*, Japanese
flower arranging; eat *baklavas*, sticky honey pastries from Greece;
paint *pysankas*, Ukrainian Easter eggs; watch the limbo, a Jamaican
dance; or find out how to put on a *sari*, an Indian dress for
women. Other cities in Canada have similar festivals each year to
celebrate the many cultures of the people who have settled the
land.

A YOUNG NATION

Canada is a young nation—it celebrated its centenary in 1967.
Although the land has been settled for hundreds of years, it was
only in 1867 that a nation called the Dominion of Canada was
formed, at first from four former British colonies. At that time, the
population of the new country was about three million people.
The ties to Britain were still strong in 1867—the new nation did
not have the right, for example, to make treaties.

Yoho National Park in British Columbia

Today, Canada is completely independent, sharing North America with the United States, Mexico, and its neighbors to the south. The queen of England is also queen of Canada, but this tie is largely ceremonial, and one that Canadians are free to reject if they decide to amend their constitution.

THE SECOND LARGEST COUNTRY

Canada is also a huge, empty land. It is the second largest country in the world, and yet has a population about one-tenth that of the United States. Of this population, only the Inuit and other Native people have lived here for more than four hundred years. Scientists believe their ancestors came to North America from Asia thousands of years ago. Europeans did not settle until the seventeenth century, and only in small numbers.

Left: An old engraving showing the harbor in the St. Lawrence River at Quebec
Right: The exact replica of the settlement at Port Royal Habitation

SETTLEMENT

The first Europeans to start permanent settlements were the French. In 1605, a settlement was attempted at Port Royal, in what is now Nova Scotia. A reconstruction of the Port Royal Habitation has been built on the site. Another settlement, beginning with the founding of Quebec in 1608, spread along the banks of the St. Lawrence River and the coast of the Gulf of St. Lawrence. From there the French moved inland along the lakes and rivers, penetrating into the present-day United States through the Ohio River valley and the Mississippi River to establish the colony of Louisiana, named in honor of the French king, Louis XIV.

In Canada today, the French imprint is strongest in the province of Quebec, though it is not confined to that province. There is a large French-speaking population in New Brunswick, and about 10 percent of the population of Prince Edward Island and Nova

Scotia are descendants of the Acadians, the name given to the French settlers in the Atlantic provinces. Manitoba and Ontario also have large French-speaking minorities.

The first large influx of English-speaking settlers came in 1783 at the end of the Revolutionary War, known in Canada as the American Revolution. In the United States, these immigrants, supporters of the British king, were called Tories. In Canada, they were known as Loyalists. About thirty thousand Loyalists, among whom were thirty-five hundred free blacks and one thousand black slaves, settled in what is now known as the Maritime provinces, particularly in present-day New Brunswick. Another ten thousand settled in Quebec and along the St. Lawrence River in what is now Ontario.

Some of the settlers who arrived from the south in 1783 were not English-speaking. A large number of Iroquois and German-speaking Mennonites from Pennsylvania (Pennsylvania Dutch) settled in southern Ontario to farm. These settlers were followed from 1800 to 1850 by a large number of immigrants from the British Isles.

By the end of the nineteenth century, the Canadian prairies were opened to settlement. The Canadian government advertised land in Europe and thousands of settlers poured in from what are now Poland, the Czech Republic, Slovakia, Hungary, and the Commonwealth of Independent States. There was also a large influx of pioneers from the United States, attracted by free land, who arrived to farm the prairies. Chinese, Japanese, and Sikh immigrants from India arrived on the West Coast to fish, build railways, and work in the forests.

In the twentieth century, immigrants have come from all over the world. In the early years, most immigration was from western,

Dancers from Greece (left) and Ukraine (right)

northern, and southern Europe. Since 1970, the number of immigrants from non-European countries has increased.

The effect of this quite recent mixing of cultures is seen even in small communities. Supermarkets in large cities sell Jamaican, East Indian, and Chinese foods. Austrian and German immigrants prepare their sausages and sauerkraut. Ukrainians still celebrate Christmas on January 6. Sikhs have built temples, and Italians and Portuguese celebrate saints' days with processions.

In recent years the Canadian government had encouraged recognition of this diversity which it called "multiculturalism." Students learned the history of the groups who had settled, their culture and experiences, and that multicultural heritage enriched their country. However, recent reform party arguments about multiculturalism are causing government rethinking on reforms.

Above left: Terry Fox on his "Marathon of Hope" in 1980
Below: Boathouses on the Newfoundland shore

Chapter 2

THE LAND
AND ITS RESOURCES

In April 1980, a young Canadian who had lost a leg to cancer set himself the goal of running from the East Coast to the West Coast of Canada. Terry Fox wanted to raise $10 million for cancer research. Today, a statue west of Thunder Bay on the Trans-Canada Highway marks the place where he stopped when the disease forced him to end his "Marathon of Hope." Four years later, nineteen-year-old Steve Fonyo, another cancer victim, dipped his artificial leg in the Atlantic Ocean at the eastern coast of Newfoundland. In May the following year, he reached the West Coast of Vancouver Island and stepped in the Pacific Ocean. He had run about five thousand miles (eight thousand kilometers).

HUGE LAND, FEW PEOPLE

Canada is the second-largest country in the world (after Russia, which is two and a half times as big). It covers 3,831,033 square miles (9,922,330 square kilometers). There are ten provinces: from the east, Newfoundland, Prince Edward Island, Nova Scotia, New Brunswick, Quebec, Ontario, Manitoba,

Saskatchewan, Alberta, and British Columbia; and two territories: the Yukon and the Northwest Territories. Three of the provinces–Quebec, Ontario, and British Columbia–are each larger than Texas and the Northwest Territories is as big as Alaska, Texas, California, Montana, and New Mexico combined. Within this vast area are some of the highest mountains in the world (Mount Logan, 19,524 feet; 5,951 meters), grassy plains, endless miles of lakes and forests, rivers, arctic wastelands, near deserts, fertile lowlands, and large cities.

This huge area is inhabited by slightly more than twenty-eight million people. Most Canadians live within 100 miles (160 kilometers) of its border with the United States. The population is scattered in pockets across the country, each pocket separated from the others by physical barriers. The people around the Great Lakes and the St. Lawrence Lowlands are separated from people of the prairies by the forests and lakes of the rugged area to the north and west, and from the coastal settlements of the Atlantic provinces by the Appalachian Mountains. The towering Rocky Mountains separate the people of coastal British Columbia from the prairies.

Where people live in Canada is determined by geography. There are six major regions in the country: the Canadian Sheild; the fertile lowlands of the St. Lawrence valley and southern Ontario; the Atlantic provinces; the Central Plains; the Western Cordillera; and the Arctic North.

THE CANADIAN SHIELD

In 1534, a French explorer, Jacques Cartier, entered the Gulf of St. Lawrence and sailed along the Labrador coast. In his journal

ARCTIC

NORTH

WESTERN CORDILLERA

CENTRAL

PLAINS

CANADIAN SHIELD

ATLANTIC PROVINCES

ST. LAWRENCE AND SOUTHERN
ONTARIO LOWLANDS

he wrote that it looked like "the land God gave Cain." There was
not, he said, a cartload of earth along the whole stretch. Cartier
was describing the Canadian Shield. The soil from this vast area
was scraped off by huge ice sheets in the last Ice Age, and
deposited in the plains of the West and the lowlands of southern
Ontario and Quebec.

The Canadian Shield is a rolling, rugged land of lakes, rushing
rivers, and marshes, stretching in a great arc around Hudson Bay.
It covers Labrador, most of Quebec and Ontario, and much of
Manitoba, Saskatchewan, and the eastern Northwest Territories.
The western edge of the shield is marked by a line of large lakes—
from the north, the Great Bear Lake, Great Slave Lake, Lake
Athabasca, and Lake Winnipeg. From there, the shield dips south
into the United States, along the northern shores of lakes Superior
and Huron, and back into part of southern Ontario. It crosses the
St. Lawrence River at the eastern outlet of Lake Ontario and again
dips into the United States to form the Adirondack Mountains in
New York State. Rapids were formed where the St. Lawrence

Lake Superior, the deepest, coldest, and largest of the Great Lakes, was created by a fault in the Canadian Shield.

River crossed the shield. In a joint effort, the United States and Canada built the St. Lawrence Seaway to drown these rapids and open the Great Lakes to seagoing ships in 1959.

In the South, where the growing season is long enough, the shield area is forested by coniferous evergreens such as the white pine and spruce. Farther north, the growing season is shorter and the trees are stunted and scattered. In the far North, it is too cold for trees, and the land is covered in the short six-week summer with mosses, short grass, and desertlike plants that grow, bloom, and fade very quickly. This is the vast area of the tundra.

The shield is an area rich in forests, animal life, hydroelectricity, and minerals, but few people live there. The soil is so poor, and the growing season so short, that farming is not practical.

THE ST. LAWRENCE AND SOUTHERN ONTARIO LOWLANDS

The greatest number of people live in the St. Lawrence valley and southern Ontario. The soil scraped from the Canadian Shield

The St. Lambert Lock (left) and grain-loading facilities at Sorel, near Montreal (above), are part of the St. Lawrence Seaway.

during the Ice Age has been deposited here, sometimes on the floor of huge lakes that have since been drained. As the climate warmed after the Ice Age, mixed forests of deciduous trees, such as maples and oaks, and coniferous trees covered the area. Some Native people cleared parts of the forest and farmed long before Europeans arrived in North America. Today, most of the forest is cleared and the rich farmlands are used for specialty crops, such as fruits and vegetables for the cities, and dairy and beef farms.

This area borders one of the greatest inland waterways of the world. Oceangoing vessels can travel from the Atlantic Ocean to the head of Lake Superior using the St. Lawrence River and the St. Lawrence Seaway — Great Lakes Waterway. This waterway moves huge quantities of grain, iron ore, and coal. The nearness of this area to the industries of the United States has made it the industrial heartland of Canada. Two of Canada's largest cities, Toronto and Montreal, as well as the capital, Ottawa, are located in this area.

Two New Brunswick towns: the restored waterfront of Saint John (left) and St. Andrews, which is at the end of a peninsula in Passamaquoddy Bay (right)

THE ATLANTIC PROVINCES

South and east of the St. Lawrence River lie the smallest provinces in Canada: Prince Edward Island, which is about the size of Delaware; New Brunswick; and Nova Scotia (meaning New Scotland). The island of Newfoundland, east of the Gulf of St. Lawrence, did not join Canada until 1949. The Atlantic provinces are part of the Appalachian Mountain area. Like Maine and Vermont, they are mostly rugged, mountainous, forested areas, with fertile lands in the valleys. Only Prince Edward Island has extensive areas of flat land.

The climate in the Atlantic provinces is milder than that of the St. Lawrence valley, with less severe winters but cooler summers. Occasional winter storms sometimes sweep up the Atlantic coast, causing sixty-foot (eighteen-meter) waves in the seas, and

Prince Edward Island, the setting of Anne of Green Gables, *is a peaceful area with low, rolling landscape.*

dropping huge quantities of snow. One such storm caused the loss of over eighty men when an oil-drilling platform overturned off the coast of Newfoundland in the winter of 1984. Fog is another hazard for shipping off the coast of Newfoundland. Fog is common when the warm Gulf Stream from the south meets the cold Labrador current from the north.

The fertile areas of the provinces, such as the Annapolis valley, Prince Edward Island, and the valley of the Saint John River, are used for farming. The Annapolis Lowlands of Nova Scotia are important for apple orchards and dairy farming. Prince Edward Island is famous for potatoes, and exports high-grade seed potatoes. Dairy and beef farming are also important. The upper Saint John River valley produces potatoes, and the lower valley is important for dairies, beef, poultry, hogs, and vegetables. With a limited amount of farmland, an important source of livelihood for the people of the Atlantic provinces is fish from the sea.

At one time, the shipbuilding industry was the main industry of Nova Scotia. The famous schooner *Bluenose* was built in 1921 at Lunenburg, Nova Scotia, and people of the provinces are often referred to as "Bluenoses." Forestry has always been important, first for lumber that was exported to Britain, and used in the shipbuilding industry, and today for pulp and paper.

The major cities of the Atlantic provinces, Halifax (Nova Scotia), Saint John (New Brunswick), Charlottetown (Prince Edward Island), and St. John's (Newfoundland) are all main ports for the area. Most other settlements hug the coast and the fertile river valleys.

THE CENTRAL PLAINS

West of the Canadian Shield and east of the Rocky Mountains lie the Central Plains, stretching as far as the Arctic Ocean in the North. Alberta, Saskatchewan, and Manitoba are sometimes known as the Prairie provinces. The French word *prairie*, meaning meadow, was used by the explorers to describe the open, grass-covered treeless plains they found when they moved west. At that time, the prairies were the home of huge herds of bison (buffalo), grizzly bears, deer, elk, moose, and other wildlife. The prairies are not flat, but a series of plains, separated by hilly escarpments, with wide, steep-sided river valleys. In the southwest, the rainfall is so scant that without irrigation the land is like a desert. One part of Alberta in this region is known as the Badlands.

In the plains north of the prairies the climate is cooler and trees are more frequent. This is known as the parkland belt. Farther north, the trees become more scattered, until they disappear and the vegetation becomes tundra.

Calgary (above), a city in Alberta; ripe, golden wheat fields (above left), near Regina; and wheat elevators (left), which are called the "cathedrals of the plains"

The northern plains are drained by a huge river—the mighty Mackenzie, the twelfth longest river in the world. The Mackenzie empties into the Arctic Ocean. The other major river of the plains—the Saskatchewan—drains into Hudson Bay.

Most people in the plains live in the prairies and the parkland belt. These are the areas where farming is possible, and where huge grain farms are located. Wheat has been an important export crop since the area was settled by farmers in the late 1890s. Since World War II, huge potash deposits have been mined in Saskatchewan, and vast deposits of petroleum and gas have been developed in Alberta and to a lesser extent in Saskatchewan. Edmonton and Winnipeg are the two largest cities. Calgary and Regina, the capital of Saskatchewan, are also important.

One of the loveliest lakes in the world, Moraine Lake in the Rockies, Alberta

THE WESTERN CORDILLERA

West of the plains lie the mountains of the Western Cordillera. The highest range in this tangle of mountains is the majestic Rockies. Approached from the east, they rise like a snowcapped wall, a formidable barrier. There are only three passes through the Rockies, and one of these is subject to avalanches that close it in winter. West of the Rockies lie more ranges that are lower, but still difficult to cross. These mountains also were affected by the Ice Age, and have been sculpted by huge glaciers. At the coast, the ice gouged deep fjords and left numerous inlets but little flat land. The chief flat area on the West Coast is the Fraser valley, a wide alluvial plain built up by the flooding river. At the mouth of the Fraser lies Vancouver, Canada's chief port.

Douglas firs on Vancouver Island, British Columbia

The climate of the West Coast of Canada is the most moderate of any part of the country. Temperatures are kept cool in winter and warm in summer by westerly winds off the Pacific Ocean. These cross a warm current and pick up moisture. As the air rises to cross the mountains, it cools, and the moisture condenses. Some parts of the coast of British Columbia have over 100 inches (254 centimeters) of rain each year. Washed by continuous moisture and favored with mild temperatures, the land is covered by dense rain forest. Trees can grow to an enormous size. Some Douglas firs are 300 feet (91 meters) tall, 13 feet (4.8 meters) in diameter, and over one thousand years old.

Inland, the air becomes drier. Some parts of British Columbia resemble a desert, with cactus plants and hardy grasses. This is because these areas are in the rain shadow of the coastal mountains. The dry, sunny interior of British Columbia is favorable for fruit growing, and the limited flatlands of the Okanagan valley are important for cherries and other fruits.

Sometimes in winter the air crossing the Rockies brings a welcome relief to the people in the foothills of the mountains of Alberta. The descending air warms and melts snow in a matter of hours. This is the famous chinook. Sometimes these warm winds raise the temperature by over forty degrees in an hour.

The northern parts of the Western Cordillera are cooler than those of the south. Inland, the temperatures in the Yukon Territory are among the coldest in North America. The lowest temperature ever recorded in Canada (minus 81.4 degrees Fahrenheit; minus 63 degrees Celsius) was measured at Snag in the Yukon. At the coast, the moderate winds from the ocean make it warmer than southern Ontario in the winter, where icy blasts from the Arctic North have been known to sweep down and bring snow in May and frost in June.

The population in the Western Cordillera is clustered in the lowlands wherever farming is possible, or in mining towns. There are rich deposits of silver, lead, coal, and other minerals in the mountains. The port of Vancouver dominates the area, and has nearly 50 percent of the population of all British Columbia and the Yukon Territory.

THE ARCTIC NORTH

Above the treeline, where it is too cold for trees to grow, is the tundra. Summer in these areas is so short that the ground never thaws fully. This condition is known as permafrost. Consequently, water from the melted snow cannot sink into the ground, and the soil is waterlogged and marshy. In areas where settlements have been made, special housing must be built to cope with the conditions.

Clockwise from top left: Inuit children from North Quebec; exposed permafrost in the Yukon Territory; Arctic tundra near Char Lake, Victoria Island, Northwest Territories; and an Eskimo fisherman, Baffin Island

North of the mainland of North America lie the Arctic islands. The largest of these, Baffin Island, is larger than California. These islands have some rich deposits of minerals. The world's northernmost mine, the Polaris mine, has been opened on Little Cornwallis Island to work the lead and zinc deposits.

The cold, windswept areas of the tundra are home to the Inuit. The Inuit traditionally lived by hunting and fishing for seals, whales, polar bears, and caribou. Now they are settled in communities, such as Cape Dorset and Inuvik.

Canada's geography poses a challenge to the people who settle the land.

Above: Saturday traffic at the Canadian-United States border in British Columbia
Below: Two bilingual signs and a marquee on a French-language theater

Chapter 3

THE PEOPLE

Visitors crossing the border from the United States into Canada or arriving at a Canadian airport are immediately aware that they are entering a country with two languages. All signs are posted in English and French. This is because Canada has two official languages. Both languages are used by the federal government and are seen throughout Canada. This bilingualism is a reflection of the history of European settlement by the British and the French.

THE FRENCH FACT

Almost one-third of Canada's population uses French as a first language. About 80 percent of the people in the province of Quebec are of French descent, but there are significant numbers of French-speaking citizens in New Brunswick, Manitoba, and Ontario.

The people of Quebec call themselves Quebecers. Some consider themselves Quebecers first and Canadians second. The province was settled by the French in the early seventeenth century. It remained a colony of France until 1763, when the British formally took it over. British rule in Quebec did not change the basic structure of society. The language, laws, and religion were maintained. British and American merchants and businessmen, however, took over much of the economic life of the colony.

Since 1960, Quebecers have taken over much of the control of their economy. A period of rapid social change and reform now called the Quiet Revolution took place between 1960 and 1966. The province's educational system was changed; hydroelectricity was nationalized; social security programs were improved; labor laws liberalized; and the state generally played a more active part in the social and economic life of the province.

A strong movement in favor of political separation from the rest of Canada grew. The Parti Quebecois, a party dedicated to negotiating a new political agreement with Canada came to power in 1976. A referendum was held in 1980 in which the people of Quebec voted not to allow the Parti Quebecois to negotiate a new relationship with the rest of Canada. Although 41.8 percent voted in favor of negotiating a new agreement, the majority rejected the proposition. In October 1995 another referendum was held, and Quebecers once again rejected the idea of separating from Canada by a slim majority of 50.6 percent.

One Canadian writer has described Canada as two solitides — meaning that English Canada and French Canada have developed separately. Throughout Canadian history there have been tensions between the two groups. In the 1990s, Quebec continued demands to be recognized as a distinct society with rights to self-government. At a constitutional conference, these rights were reaffirmed, along with promoting linguistic duality. Council plans for unity were scrapped for rethinking of solutions.

THE ENGLISH FACT

Before 1900, most immigrants to Canada came from the British Isles. They brought with them their traditions of government, language, and customs. They were proud of their connection with Britain. When the Confederation of Canada was formed in 1867, these ties were reinforced by Canada's retention of the monarchy and the British parliamentary institutions.

Today, Canada has its own national anthem and its own flag. Direct British cultural influence has declined to a large extent, while influence from the United States has increased. Yet visitors who go to both Canada and the United States perceive noticeable differences between the two countries.

THE NATIVE PEOPLE

The Native people are the original inhabitants of Canada, having lived in what is now Canada for at least ten thousand years. Most of the Native people lived by hunting, fishing, trading, and gathering. Farming groups lived in communities in southern Ontario and the St. Lawrence lowlands.

The coming of the Europeans meant great changes for these people. They had no immunity to diseases such as measles, smallpox, and colds, which were carried by the seamen and traders. No one knows how many thousands died.

In the North, the Inuit had the earliest contact with Europeans. It is believed that the Vikings contacted them in the eleventh century. In the 1500s and 1600s, British seamen such as Martin Frobisher, John Davis, and Henry Hudson entered the sea lanes, searching for a sailing route to the riches of the East. The Inuit were hunters and gatherers, and traded with the Europeans. They acted as guides to explorers, showing them how to survive in the difficult environment. The Inuit have mainly given up their nomadic life and have settled in communities, but their culture remains strong. They have taken an increasingly active role in determining their future. After 15 years of negotiations with Ottawa, an agreement was announced in 1991, under which the Inuit would take political control of one-fifth of Canada's land area. The new territory called *Nunavut*, "Our Land," would be comprised of the eastern two-thirds of the Northwest Territories where 17,500 Inuit live. The Inuit are to gain additional mineral rights but will give up other mineral claims in exchange for $1 billion. Some natives claim that this settlement undermines their demand for total self-government. When the accord is finalized, the designation "Northwest Territories" will disappear from Canadian maps. Finalization is set for 1999.

Introduction of the fur trade by Europeans caused competition between Native people for tools and trade goods. Huron farmers and traders were wiped out by Iroquois from the south and diseases. Today, many Iroquois of Canada, known as the Six Nations, are descendants of groups from the United States who were granted land by the British after the American War for Independence. The relationship between Europeans and Native people altered the traditional way of life. People became more dependent on European trade goods but were able to retain much of their culture. Fur traders often married native women whose descendants formed a third group, English or French-speaking Metis. Extermination of buffalo by hide hunters from the United States by the 1880s left the Native and Metis hunters with no food base. So the Canadian government made treaties with Native people promising land, food, education, and aid with farms even when forestland was not farmed. Often children were taken and sent away for training in European religions, French, or English.

Native people in traditional costumes

On the West Coast, Native people were skilled carvers who lived in large family homes made with logs from huge trees in the area. Traders came from Russia, New England, and Britain for sea otter skins to trade in China. Along with metal tools that facilitated Native art, they also brought devastating disease.

The Native culture, however, was too strong to be destroyed. Since the 1970s, Native people have been challenging the terms of the original treaties. Their culture has become a source of pride, and paintings, sculptures, carvings, and prints by Native artists are collectors' items. Other Canadians are supporting them in their efforts to prevent thoughtless development of their fragile environments. In 1986, for example, a group of Haida from British Columbia traveled across Canada to try to prevent the logging of islands that were their ancestral land. The government of British Columbia had given permission to loggers to harvest trees that were over one thousand years old. Environmentalists described

Totem poles are a unique art form practiced by the Northwest Pacific Coast Indians. They are carved of cedar wood and show a crest or sign of a family or clan, similar to coats-of-arms. This is a Haida totem pole.

the islands as a Canadian Galapagos because of the unique plant life. Other Canadians joined the Haida in questioning the decision.

In the current Northwest Territories, whose name designation will change, Native people number about 50 percent of the population. The greatest number live in Ontario. The total Native population, including the Metis, was estimated to be some 586,000 in 1991. As these people continue to demand a voice in governing their own affairs, there are numerous signs that they are being heard.

OTHER GROUPS

In 1901, about 90 percent of the Canadian population had French or British origins. Today more than 30 percent have non-French and non-British origins. More than thirty-five different ethnic groups are represented in this mix. Immigration of some of these groups is so recent that at least 1.6 million people in Canada do not speak English or French.

The larger cities in Canada reflect this mixing. Some of the ethnic groups live close together in neighborhoods. In the prairies, where whole blocks of land were settled by immigrants from one area of Europe, the language has survived several generations. The policy of multiculturalism, the acceptance of many cultures, came about as these people asked that their contribution to the culture of Canada be recognized.

REGIONALISM

Within Canada there are strong feelings of regional differences from one part of the country to another.

The settlement pattern was a reflection of geography — the areas of lowland and plain that can be settled are separated from each other by mountains or the bare rocky shield. The result was that each pocket of settlement developed separately, and often in comparative isolation from other areas. This meant, for example, that the French settlement that developed in Nova Scotia, around the Bay of Fundy, was separate and different from the French settlement that developed in the St. Lawrence lowlands. The first farming settlement in the prairies around the site of what is now Winnipeg was different from the farming settlements in southern Ontario, both in the people who settled there and the experiences they had.

Regionalism is important in Canada because it means that each area has a strong sense of its past and interests. In recent years, this has led to political movements in Quebec and in the West to protect these interests. Each part of Canada, in effect, has a different outlook and culture. This makes it very difficult to make generalizations about the country and its people.

Chapter 4

CANADA BEFORE CONFEDERATION

THE FIRST SETTLERS

Thousands of years ago, most of Canada was covered by huge ice sheets centered on Hudson Bay and the western mountains. For at least two periods between thirty-six thousand and thirteen thousand years ago, scientists believe conditions changed enough for there to be a land bridge between Asia and North America. Animals, followed by the people who hunted them, crossed the land bridge and moved through the mountains and Central Plains. These people are thought to be the ancestors of the Native people.

Much knowledge of how the Native people lived before the coming of the Europeans has been lost. At the time of contact, there were many different groups. The people on the West Coast lived by fishing, hunting, and gathering food and supplies from the land around them. One group, called by the Europeans the Nootka, hunted whales in the Pacific. Food was so plentiful that those groups lived in permanent settlements of solid wooden

Opposite page: Angel Glacier in Jasper National Park, Alberta,
gives us an idea of how Canada might have looked thousands of years ago.

Left: Pictographs drawn by early settlers
Right: Fish are as plentiful today as they were for the early settlers.

houses. In the mountains, where food was less plentiful, the people lived from the salmon that migrated to the rivers and lakes and from food that could be gathered from the land. They were nomadic, which means they moved during the year, collecting food in a regular pattern. Winters were usually spent in sheltered valleys in homes with floors dug below ground level for greater warmth.

In the prairies, groups lived by hunting buffalo, deer, and other game. They built pounds to capture the animals or drove them over cliffs. These people were also nomadic. They stored meat from a successful hunt by drying it in strips and then pounding it between stones until it became like a powder. The meat was then mixed with fat and flavored with dried fruit, such as the saskatoon berry, and stored in bags made of buffalo stomachs. This was very concentrated food, but easy to carry from place to place. The fur traders who came later traded with the people for this food, which was called pemmican. Before the use of horses, the plains Indians used dogs to help carry their possessions. They lived in tents, called tipis, made from buffalo hides.

To the north and east of the prairies, in the coniferous forest, the people lived from the land, hunting, fishing, and gathering food. They made shelters from skins or bark mats stretched over a wooden framework. Food was more difficult to obtain in this area, and for much of the year people lived as small family groups. To the north of the forest group lived the Inuit, who came to North America in waves of settlement starting over four thousand years ago. In this harsh environment, the Inuit lived by hunting caribou or, on the coast, by hunting seals and fishing. Survival was difficult, and for most of the year the people spent their time gathering food. Their winter homes were made of ice blocks or, if they were close to the coast, of driftwood and skins. In summer, when the land was free of ice and snow, they used skin tents.

In the Great Lakes area and St. Lawrence valley, the climate was warm enough for corn, squash, tobacco, and beans to grow. The groups who lived in this area were related to the Iroquois. They lived in large settled villages, cultivating the surrounding lands and trading. As the soil became exhausted, the villages were moved. The people lived in longhouses, made of birch or elm bark mats stretched over a wooden framework. Several related families lived in one house. Recent excavations in southern Ontario have shown houses that were as long as 150 feet (45.7 meters). The villages were surrounded by high wooden fences for protection from attacks. These people traded corn for meat and skins with the people of the north.

On the East Coast, the people lived from fish, deer, and other game. Like all the other Native people, their tools were made of

Left: A portrait of Jacques Cartier
Right: The remains of a Norse settlement from about A.D. 1000
have been excavated in L'Anse Aux Meadows, Newfoundland.

stone, bone, or wood. They were nomadic and lived in shelters
made of skins or mats spread over a wooden framework. They
were the first to encounter the Europeans and in some cases, they
disappeared altogether in the face of diseases and warfare. The
coming of the Europeans with metal tools, woven clothes, and
domestic animals, such as cattle and horses, changed their lives.

NEW FRANCE

The first European contact in Canada was made by Vikings
from Greenland. Archaeologists have excavated a site on the
island of Newfoundland that was briefly settled by these seafaring
warriors. In the late fifteenth century, the fishing banks off
Newfoundland and the Gulf of St. Lawrence were visited by
Basque, Portuguese, English, and Breton fishermen.

After Cartier's visit in 1534, the eastern coast was frequently
visited by merchants and fishermen from Europe who came for
the cod. Whaling stations were built along the shores of the St.
Lawrence and Labrador coast by the Basques. They traded iron

Samuel de Champlain is considered the founder of New France.

tools and cloth with the Native people, taking in return their well worn and old beaver skin robes. At that time, felt hats made from beaver skins were the rage for fashionable European men. The prospect of fortunes to be made in the fur trade caused the French to turn again to the lands along the St. Lawrence.

The first attempt at settlement was made at Port Royal in the Annapolis valley, part of what is now Nova Scotia. The attempt ended in 1613 when a British expedition from Virginia burned the settlement. The second attempt in 1608 by Samuel de Champlain at Quebec on the St. Lawrence River was successful.

Slowly, under the guiding hand of Champlain, the settlement of St. Lawrence grew. Although Champlain encouraged farmers, the lifeblood of the settlement was the fur trade. The Native people to the north and the Hurons, a branch of the Iroquois to the west, traded with the French. They acted as middlemen, bringing beaver furs from the shield area to the shores of the St. Lawrence. Champlain helped these people in their wars against the Mohawks and other Iroquois of what is now New York. For nearly one hundred years, the small settlements along the St. Lawrence were engaged in fierce battle for control of this area.

Within seven years of the founding of Quebec, Roman Catholic missionaries arrived. They went into the country of the Hurons to learn their way of life and to try to convert them to Christianity. They brought with them European diseases, such as measles and smallpox. The Hurons died in the hundreds from these diseases. Their traditional society was undermined. Weakened, the Hurons were overrun and wiped out by the Iroquois in 1649, and the missionaries' outposts were burned to the ground. The settlement at Montreal, which had been founded by missionaries, became a defense outpost. The colony was in danger of disappearing. In this crisis, the French king sent an able administrator to the colony. Jean Talon was only in New France for seven years, but in that time he set up industries, schools, a militia (civilian army), and brought in hundreds of settlers.

New France was settled by a seigneurial system, which was modeled on the landholding system used in France. The king granted land to a seigneur, who was responsible for clearing the land and bringing in settlers. The settlers then paid rent to the seigneur. The seigneuries were laid out along the banks of the rivers and the first settlers had long narrow lots fronting the water.

Yet the fur trade was still the lifeblood of New France. Young men who wanted to make their fortunes took to the woods to become traders. They penetrated far into the interior of North America, searching out Native people who had not traded directly with Europeans before. The authorities in New France tried to stop the young men from leaving for the woods.

Two of the traders, Pierre Radisson and Sieur des Groseilliers, were imprisoned and fined for illegal trading. Their furs were taken from them when they returned to the St. Lawrence after a two-year absence in 1669. The two went to the British and told them of the rich furs around Hudson Bay. King Charles II of England was interested. In 1670, Groseilliers and one small ship, the *Nonsuch*, sailed into the bay and came back to England with a load of furs that made the backers of the expedition rich. The king gave a charter to the company, now known as the Hudson's Bay Company.

Slowly, despite attacks from the French, the English established fur trade posts along the shores of Hudson Bay. It was inevitable that the English and French would clash in North America. For over a hundred years they had been at war in Europe. The Seven Years' War (the French and Indian Wars) broke out in North America in 1756, when the French laid claim to lands in the Ohio valley that were also claimed by the Thirteen Colonies. At the end of the war, the French had been defeated, and New France became a British colony.

BRITISH COLONIES

In the years after the conquest, the British agreed that the French could keep their language, their church, and their laws, including the landholding system. When the American Revolution began in 1775, the colony, although invaded by American forces, remained loyal to the British. The Canadians, as the settlers were known, believed that they had more chance to retain their culture under the British than as part of the new United States.

With the end of the war in 1783, about forty thousand settlers came to the British colonies from the United States. In the Maritimes, the population increased so much that the British decided to make two new colonies, New Brunswick and Cape Breton (now part of Nova Scotia). Other settlers went to the eastern townships, the area of southern Quebec close to the boundary with the United States. About seventy-five hundred settled in southern Ontario.

The coming of the settlers from the south changed the face of the land. The new settlers were used to living under a British form of government, with an assembly, where they were represented. They were not prepared to live under a system of laws based on the French tradition. The single colony of Canada was split into two sections in 1791, Upper Canada (which is now Ontario) and Lower Canada (now Quebec). Settlers started to come from Britain to settle in the new colonies. In the Canadas, canals were built and railways started. The sound of the broad ax echoed throughout the Ottawa valley as the huge white pines were felled to be sent to England for use as pit props in the coal mines. In the Maritimes, a shipbuilding industry flourished. In the 1860s, one-quarter of the shipping tonnage in the world was built in Nova Scotian shipyards. The population was rising and industry was booming.

Canada was becoming wary of its neighbor to the south. In the war of 1812, the United States declared war on Britain and attacked the colonies. In Upper Canada, the lowly capital of York, known for many years as Muddy York, was burned. In retaliation, the British sailed up the Potomac and burned the presidential mansion. With a handful of British troops and the local militia, the Canadians were able to turn back the invaders along the Niagara frontier and in the eastern townships.

FUR TRADE IN THE WEST

After the British took over New France, the Hudson's Bay Company was challenged by traders working out of Montreal.

Reenactment of the voyageurs' journey in 1775

Gradually these traders forced the company to move inland. In 1775, the Northwest Company was formed by the challengers. They loaded 36-foot (10.9-meter) canoes with trade goods at Montreal, and for six weeks paddled and portaged along the Ottawa River, the French River, Lake Huron, and the north shore of Lake Superior to their depot at the head of the lake. There they met up with traders who had come from the distant trading posts along the Saskatchewan rivers and the north. These traders were the wintering partners who lived and traded in the northwest. The *voyageurs*, the paddlers of the canoes, were usually French-speaking men from Lower Canada. They and the traders intermarried with Indian women. Their descendants today are the French-speaking Metis.

The fur traders explored the west, searching for a route to the Pacific Ocean. Their names are remembered in the Mackenzie

Left: The Thompson River valley in British Columbia
Right: A restored Hudson's Bay Company store

River, named for Alexander Mackenzie, the first white man to cross the North American continent; the Fraser River, named after Simon Fraser; and the Thompson River in British Columbia, named for David Thompson.

The rivalry between the two fur companies broke into warfare in 1819. The Hudson's Bay Company had claimed the area around what is now Winnipeg. They had granted this land to Lord Selkirk, a Scottish earl who planned to bring settlers to the Red River area and give them land to farm. The first settlers arrived in 1812. Metis lived in the area and sold pemmican to the traders. They viewed the settlers as trespassers who would drive the buffalo away. The fur traders were also opposed to the settlement. In 1819, the Metis and settlers clashed. Nineteen settlers died and the homes of the remaining·people were burned to the ground. The disputes were ended when the two companies joined forces in 1821. Slowly, the settlement at Red River prospered until by 1860 there were about five thousand people: retired fur traders and their children, Scottish settlers, and English-speaking Metis.

A gold mine in British Columbia

THE WEST COAST

The Spaniards were the first Europeans to claim the West Coast of Canada. In 1798, they gave up these claims in favor of the British. Traders from the United States and Britain visited the area to buy furs and supplies from the people of the coast. The British government granted the area to the Hudson's Bay Company after a boundary treaty was made with the United States in 1846.

The West Coast remained a quiet backwater until gold was found in the Fraser valley in 1858. Thousands of miners and fortune seekers from California and around the world poured into what is now British Columbia. In 1860, a gold strike in the Cariboo resulted in a stampede to the inland areas. Britain took over the territory from the Hudson's Bay Company and made James Douglas, the chief trader in the area, governor. Douglas almost single-handedly kept control of the area. He forced the miners to buy licenses, and within a year a police force and justice system were in place. With the help of Judge Matthew Begbie, over 6-feet (1.8-meters) tall and known locally as the hanging judge, Douglas brought law and order to the frontier.

An engraving entitled Timber Depot near Quebec, *made by William Henry Bartlett on his travels through Canada in 1842.*

BEGINNINGS OF CONFEDERATION

By 1867, the colonies of eastern British North America were in difficulties. They needed markets for their chief products: grain, lumber, and fish. The situation was made very difficult in 1866 when the United States ended a trade treaty between itself and the colonies.

There also was a political deadlock in the Province of Canada. In 1838, small rebellions in Upper and Lower Canada had broken out in protest against the system of government. Both sections felt they were not adequately represented in the legislative assemblies. They felt cultural and religious differences were not being addressed. Some talked of adopting a republican government, or even of joining the United States. The rebellions were put down, but in the aftermath Upper and Lower Canada again were joined.

They were known as Canada East and Canada West. The system did not work, and by 1860, the political strains were severe.

CONFEDERATION

There were economic reasons, too, for the Province of Canada to press for unity with the other colonies. Businessmen in Canada West wanted to expand into the west. The railway building era was well underway, and merchants wanted to open the western lands for farming.

Moreover, the British colonies were aware of how powerful the United States was in military strength. During the Civil War years, there was talk in the United States of annexing the lands to the north. After the North won the Civil War, the colonists had even more to fear. The colonies had a better chance of withstanding invasion if they were united. This feeling was reinforced during the talks that led to unity, or Confederation, when Irish sympathizers, called Fenians, raided the colonies from across the U.S. border.

The solution to the problems was to make one country out of the colonies. Britain encouraged the movement for economic reasons. There was much less enthusiasm for the idea of Confederation in the Maritimes than in the Province of Canada. Prince Edward Island and Newfoundland decided not to join in 1867. There was strong opposition in Nova Scotia and in New Brunswick. But the British Parliament passed the Confederation agreement in 1867, uniting Upper Canada (to be called Ontario), Lower Canada (to be called Quebec), New Brunswick, and Nova Scotia in a federal union.

Bartlett's engraving shows Bytown around 1840, renamed Ottawa in 1854.

Under the agreement, the queen of England was also queen of the federal union, and a parliamentary system of government similar to the one in Britain was approved. Steps were taken to pave the way for the other British-held areas in North America to become part of the Canadian state. The capital was to be Ottawa, a small insignificant lumbering town once known as Bytown, on the Ottawa River. Once again the United States influenced the choice. Ottawa was chosen by Queen Victoria because it was far enough from the border to be safe from attack by the increasingly powerful neighbor.

Chapter 5

FROM SEA TO SEA

Canada's motto, translated from Latin, means "From sea to sea." The original Confederation was made up of only four of the former British colonies—Nova Scotia, New Brunswick, and the two Canadas (East and West). It was 1871 before the new country stretched from sea to sea. In 1869, Canada purchased the claims of the Hudson's Bay Company to the western lands.

Manitoba had joined Canada in 1870, but not before an uprising by the Metis. No effort was made by the Canadian government to assure the Metis at the Red River settlement that their culture or their claims to the land would be recognized. Surveyors, sent from the east, ignored the Metis property lines in their work. Louis Riel, the spokesman for the Metis, was made head of a provisional government set up by representatives elected by the settlers. The new government was to negotiate terms of entry into Confederation with Canada. In March 1870, Riel allowed the execution of Thomas Scott, an Irish immigrant to Canada who had strong Protestant and anti-Catholic sympathies, and who had plotted to assassinate Riel. British and Canadian troops were sent in August 1870 to restore order, and Riel fled the new province.

*The Great Seal of the
Dominion of Canada
adopted after the Confederation
of 1867*

The Metis' rights were overshadowed by the mass of settlers who moved west. Treaties were made with the Native people on the plains. British Columbia entered the Confederation in 1871 on the promise that the Canadian government would build a railway across the continent to link it to the east.

The other eastern colonies, Prince Edward Island and Newfoundland, still were not interested in joining the new country. In 1873, the Prince Edward Island railway was in financial difficulties. In return for a promise to cover its debt, it agreed to join the Confederation. Newfoundland did not join until 1949.

THE BUILDING OF THE RAILWAY

In 1871, the fastest overland route to the new province of British Columbia was by the transcontinental railroad through the United States. By sea, the journey was around the tip of South America or through the isthmus of Panama. To reach Manitoba in 1870 using an all-Canadian route, troops from the east had to travel by canoe, following the old voyageurs from the head of Lake Superior to the Red River. If Canada was to be a nation

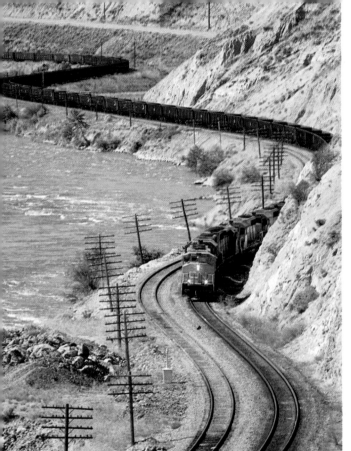

A modern-day freight train (left) and the first passenger train in the Yukon, 1899 (right)

stretching from sea to sea, a railway link through Canadian territory had to be built.

Finally the last spike was driven and the line was opened in 1885. From the beginning there were problems in raising the needed money. The difficulties of building through the rugged shield were immense and the process expensive. Machines were swallowed by marsh and swamps. Ancient granite rocks had to be blasted to make a flat bed for the rails. Thousands of workers were needed. The contractor hired to build the line through the mountains of the west employed Chinese labor. Some estimates of the casualties suffered by the Chinese along the worst stretches were one dead man for each tie laid. The line ended in the new town of Vancouver, destined, because of this choice, to become Canada's largest city on the West Coast.

THE SETTLEMENT OF THE WEST

The Mounties—the Royal Canadian Mounted Police—have become, like the beaver and the maple leaf, a symbol of Canada. The Mounties were formed in 1873 in response to a plea by the Indians of the western plains. Whiskey traders from south of the border were selling home-brewed liquor to the tribes of the Plains, and their leaders wanted help in bringing law and order to the area. In 1874, a volunteer group of horsemen set out from Winnipeg to southern Alberta. They wore red jackets, as the Indians trusted this symbol of British soldiers. Their ride is remembered as the Long March, as it was two months before they reached their destination. The Mounties stationed one or two men in each fort in the west and kept law and order over a vast territory that eventually extended to the Arctic shores.

The building of the railroad did not bring an immediate flood of settlers to the prairies. It did, however, lead to rebellion in the west. Many Metis left the Red River area as settlers from the east poured in. They moved into lands in what is now Saskatchewan and Alberta. The Canadian government was slow to recognize their land claims, even though they made land deals with the railway company and negotiated treaties with the Native people. Frustrated, the Metis, under the leadership of Louis Riel, took up arms. The rebellion was quickly put down with some difficulty and Riel was executed.

By the mid-1890s the last of the best free land was taken in the United States. The Canadian Pacific Railway (CPR), finished in 1885, had opened the prairies. A new strain of rust-resistant wheat that could ripen in the short growing season of the Canadian prairies had been developed. A good price for wheat

Left: The Royal Canadian Mounted Police
Right: Traveling in 1898 to the Klondike gold rush

and falling costs for transportation of the grain to Europe meant that farmers could make a living by growing and selling grain. The Canadian government advertised in Europe for farmers. Thousands of Americans moved northward. By 1905, the best of the land was settled, and wheat became the chief export crop.

The Canadian government had promoted a policy it hoped would bring about growth. The idea behind the national policy, as it was called, was that the west would provide grain for export. The farmers in the west would require machinery and consumer goods that would be made in the east. This exchange would create a national economy and help the whole of Canada to prosper.

OPENING THE NORTH

Mining has always been a factor in the development of Canada's north. The true extent of the world's largest nickel deposit at Sudbury in northern Ontario was discovered when the CPR mainline was being built through the area in 1883. The Klondike gold rush to the Yukon Territory in 1897 brought

100,000 gold seekers to the area. This discovery made many southern Canadians aware of their northern lands for the first time. Men sent by the Geological Survey of Canada mapped and surveyed the area and discovered mineral deposits. By the 1930s, bush planes were flying from Edmonton, linking the scattered miner's settlements along the Mackenzie.

INDEPENDENCE FROM BRITAIN

Confederation did not mark Canada's independence from Britain. Foreign relations and treaties with other countries, for example, were conducted through the governor-general, by the British foreign office, and by its ambassadors. Gradually, Canadians won the right to make their own decisions. The Canadians decided to form their own navy in 1910, rather than contribute to the British navy.

In World War I, the Canadian government supported Britain in the war against Germany and its allies, and sent troops overseas. At this time, Canada had a population of about 8 million, yet during the war had about 600,000 men in uniform. The Canadian troops distinguished themselves in several battles. At Ypres, Belgium, in 1915, they fought with British troops to hold back a German attack that involved the first use of chlorine gas. In 1917 at Vimy Ridge, France, they captured a hill that had been held by German troops against massive assaults by British and French troops. The Canadian Corps, which launched this attack and another successful offensive at Passchendaele, Belgium, was an elite fighting unit. Canadian troops paid a high price in casualties—about 60,000 men were killed, and 120,000 were maimed or injured. In return for this contribution, Prime Minister

The national war memorial in Ottawa

Robert Borden expected and was given a voice in the decisions being made on the conduct of the war. With the coming of peace, Canada was recognized as an autonomous nation, and by 1931 achieved full independence.

THE GREAT DEPRESSION

The Great Depression started in 1929 and lasted until the outbreak of World War II in 1939. It was a traumatic time for Canada, especially for the western provinces, where droughts also devastated the area. One person out of five was dependent on the government for relief. The western provinces relied on exports, especially wheat, but also on minerals and forest products. By

1933, two-thirds of the farm families in Saskatchewan were on relief. Droughts, crop failures, and low prices for wheat technically bankrupted the province.

Pulp and paper had become Canada's major export in the 1920s. The industry was particularly important in Ontario and Quebec, where some companies went bankrupt. Unemployment reached record levels in Ontario and Quebec.

The Maritime provinces suffered from the Great Depression also. Because the depression was worldwide, a sharp drop in foreign trade left many unemployed in factories and in the shipping industry.

CANADA SINCE WORLD WAR II

Canada declared war on Germany one week after the invasion of Poland in September 1939. Canadians fought in Hong Kong, North Africa, Sicily, and mainland Italy, France, and Belgium, and in the Normandy invasion. After Normandy, they went to liberate The Netherlands. Over one million men and women served in the forces, and more than forty-two thousand died. Canadian industries boomed as factories turned out planes, munitions, tanks, and cargo carriers. At the end of the war, Canada was recognized as a middle-sized power in the world.

Canada joined the United Nations in 1945. Canadian troops have supplied peace-keeping forces in the Middle East, Africa, and Asia. With the growth of the Cold War, the government joined the North Atlantic Treaty Organization (NATO) and cooperated with the United States in building a radar warning line across Canada. This was strengthened in 1954 with the DEW line from Alaska to Baffin Island in 1957. In the same year, Canada signed the

Canada is a member of international organizations and plays a prominent part in world events. An early meeting (above) of NATO in Ottawa

NORAD, the North American Air Defence Agreement, by which the air defenses of Canada and the United States were integrated. Today, NORAD also monitors aircraft suspected of drug smuggling.

With the end of the war, Canada entered a prosperous era. The federal government undertook social welfare programs. Canada now has a universal medical plan, a national pension scheme, unemployment insurance, and a system of family allowances. Immigrants poured into the country from Europe, and later from Asia, South America, and Africa. By the 1980s, more immigrants came from non-European countries than from anywhere else. Industry grew and more resources of the north were developed.

Canada continues to face challenges in the 1990s. Some provinces and regions of the country are more prosperous than others. Political groups continue to talk of separation and self-government while other provinces stress a unified Canada with one language and culture. The government, to be successful, must always be aware of provincial diversities and interests.

A Canadian gold coin, showing a portrait of Queen Elizabeth II, minted in 1980 and the Parliament buildings in Ottawa

Chapter 6

CANADA'S GOVERNMENT

Most tourists who visit Ottawa, Canada's capital city, include the Parliament buildings in their list of places to see. These buildings are the seat of the national government.

The constitution of Canada describes Parliament as including the queen, the Senate, and the House of Commons. Most Canadians do not think of the queen as being part of Parliament. This is because the queen and her representatives, the governors-general and lieutenant governors, do not use the powers they have. Canada's upper house is an appointed body called the Senate. When Canadians talk about Parliament, however, they usually mean the lower house, the House of Commons.

THE HOUSE OF COMMONS

There are five rows of desks on each side of a center aisle in the chamber of the House of Commons. At the north end of the aisle is an ornate chair, called the Speaker's chair. Above the chair is a gallery, where the public can sit to listen to the proceedings. When Parliament is sitting, the desks, called benches, are occupied by the members of Parliament, or MPs. Each of the members represents a constituency or voting district, elected by receiving the largest number of votes. In 1996 there were 295 members. Under the Constitution Act, 1986, the distribution of seats is proportionate to the populations of all the provinces.

Desks on the west side of the chamber are occupied by members of the governing political party. This is the party that won the largest number of seats in a general election. The head of this party is the prime minister. The prime minister sits in the front row surrounded by members of the cabinet. In the parliamentary system, the prime minister and cabinet are the executive branch of government that decides on policy. This system differs from the United States where the executive, the president and cabinet, do not sit in the lawmaking Congress. Members of the Canadian cabinet are elected MPs or they can be members of the Senate.

Benches on the east side of the Chamber are occupied by MPs who are not members of the governing party. Opposite the prime minister sits the leader of the opposition surrounded by MPs. The leader of the opposition is the head of the political party with the second-largest number of elected MPs.

Forty-five minutes are set aside each day for Question Period. At this time, the prime minister and members of the cabinet must answer questions asked by members of the House. Usually the questions concern government policies or issues that have been raised by the press. Question Period is at the heart of the parliamentary system of government. Here the executive must, on a daily basis, answer to the elected representatives for its actions.

All questions must be put through the Speaker, whose job it is to see that the rules of the House are followed. In addressing one another, the MPs use titles, not names, so that an MP is addressed as "the honorable member for (the constituency name)." The Speaker, an elected MP, is voted for by ballot by House members. The Speaker is expected to be impartial. The title of Speaker comes from the British Parliament, where the early members of the House of Commons chose one of their number to speak to the monarch on their behalf.

THE PRIME MINISTER AND CABINET

The constitution of Canada does not mention the prime minister or the cabinet. There is no doubt, though, that the prime minister is the most powerful political figure in the country. The office of prime minister dates from the mid-eighteenth century in Britain. The position evolved gradually, so that today many unwritten rules apply to people who occupy this office. The prime minister by tradition is an elected MP, and the leader of the political party with the most seats in the House of Commons.

The prime minister chooses the cabinet. The cabinet initiates and decides on policies and on the public bills that are to be introduced in the House of Commons. In selecting the cabinet, the prime minister takes into consideration the ethnic, religious, and regional composition of Canada. If one region of the country has not elected any MPs from the governing party, the prime minister usually chooses a member of the Senate to represent that area in the cabinet.

As long as the governing party can obtain a majority of votes in the House of Commons, bills can be passed into law. If the governing party does not have a majority of seats, as sometimes happens, a minority government is formed. The government then has to depend on the support of the opposition members to

The interior of the office of the governor-general

remain in power. Without this support, the government cannot pass legislation. If a major item, such as the budget, is defeated in the House, the government resigns, and a general election is held.

THE SENATE

The Senate, the upper house of the Canadian Parliament, has the same name as the American upper house. Its role, however, is very different. Senators are not elected, but are appointed by the governor-general on the advice of the prime minister. At one time the appointments were for life, but senators appointed since 1965 must retire at age seventy-five.

The Senate, with 104 members, is a house of regional representation. The Maritimes (Prince Edward Island, New Brunswick, and Nova Scotia), Quebec, Ontario, the western provinces (Manitoba, Saskatchewan, Alberta, and British Columbia) each have twenty-four senators; Newfoundland has six; and each territory (Yukon and current Northwest) has one. This ensures that all areas of Canada have representation. In 1867, when the Senate was set up, the smaller provinces were afraid that the views of the more populous areas, Ontario and Quebec, would dominate in Parliament.

The Senate can initiate bills, but not those involving taxes or how money should be spent. The senators debate bills passed by the House of Commons and propose amendments. These amendments must then pass the House of Commons before they are accepted. One important function of the Senate is to examine issues and present reports to the House of Commons. In 1971, for instance, the Senate produced a report on poverty that provided material for action in the House of Commons.

There is an ongoing discussion in Canada about reform of the Senate. Many of the people are appointed by the prime minister as a reward for political services, such as helping organize election campaigns or raising funds. A Senate change requires a change in the constitution. In 1991, the Citizen's Forum on Canada's Future started sounding public opinion on constitutional change.

THE CROWN

Canada is a monarchy, which means that it has a king or queen as the head of state. The monarch, however, does not exercise power in the government. All the historic powers and privileges of the Crown are held in Canada by the governor-general. At one time, the governor-general was a British representative of the monarch. Since 1952, all governors-general have been Canadian.

Although the queen of England makes the appointment, the prime minister chooses the governor-general. The appointment usually lasts for between five and seven years. It has been a practice to alternate the office between English-speaking and

Governor-general Jeanne Sauve (1984-89) bestows the Order of Canada on a deserving citizen.

French-speaking persons. In 1984, Jeanne Sauve became the first woman to be appointed governor-general.

Despite the appearance of power, the governor-general cannot interfere in partisan politics. Like the British monarch, the governor-general is above politics and must be impartial in all public actions. He or she occupies an office that is largely ceremonial. For Canada, with its diverse population and regional differences, the governor-general symbolizes unity.

THE PROVINCIAL GOVERNMENTS

Because Canada is a federation, each of the provinces has its own government. The structure of these governments is similar to that of the federal government except that there is only one legislative house; each province has a lieutenant-governor who represents the Crown. The lieutenant-governor is appointed by the governor-general on the advice of the prime minister. The provincial executive is made up of a premier and executive

The Alberta Legislative building in Edmonton

council, which is like the federal cabinet. Each legislative assembly is made up of the elected members, usually from two or more political parties.

The constitution of Canada sets out the division of powers between the federal government and the provincial governments. The federal government is responsible for matters that affect the country as a whole, such as defense, treaties, policies affecting the nation, and the printing of money. Most local matters, such as schools, are the responsibility of the provincial governments.

MUNICIPAL GOVERNMENT

Under the constitution, all the powers of the local, or municipal, governments are derived from the provincial governments. This third level of government provides services such as garbage pickup and local road maintenance. The provincial government provides funds, mainly from property taxes, to the municipal governments, and has the power to override any of the actions of

The Changing of the Guard at the Citadel in Quebec City

these governments. The municipal governments are made up of mayors, who are elected, and elected councils.

THE CONSTITUTION ACT, 1982

In 1982, the Canadian constitution was changed. A Charter of Rights is included in the new constitution. Since 1982, judges have been asked to determine whether laws passed by Parliament violate the Charter of Rights. If they do, the Supreme Court can declare these laws invalid.

THE ROLE OF GOVERNMENT

Government plays an important part in the lives of all Canadians. This is not only because the government provides important services, such as roads, or because of regulations, such as the paying of taxes. The federal government has always taken

Two Crown corporations are Air Canada and Canadian National Railways.

an important part in shaping the country, from helping private interests build the first transcontinental railways to giving Canadian artists and writers grants of money in recent years.

The federal and provincial governments can set up Crown corporations, which are wholly owned by the government, to carry out programs. The Cabinet exercises control over these bodies.

The first Crown corporation in the Province of Canada in 1841 was set up to construct a canal system. Several of the largest Crown corporations (Air Canada, Canadian National Railways, Petro-Canada), are concerned with transportation. This is because the task of providing transportation facilities in such a large country with a scattered population is too expensive for private firms to undertake. Crown corporations are also involved in some industries. For example, in most provinces, the generation and transmission of electric power is the responsibility of Crown corporations.

Canada is rich in natural resources. Mining is the principal industry
in the Yukon. At Faro (above left) is a lead-zinc mine. Gypsum is ready
to be shipped at the port of Montreal (above right). Roberts Bank
coal port in the Fraser Estuary, British Columbia (below)

Chapter 7

HOW PEOPLE MAKE THEIR LIVING

Canada is a modern industralized country, and its people earn their living in many ways. At the beginning of the twentieth century, over half of the people worked on farms or in forests and mines. Today only a small percentage of the population earns a livelihood in this way. As in the United States and other industrialized countries, the largest number of people work in service industries—in stores, banks, offices, hospitals, schools, and so on. Over 70 percent of the labor force works in service industries and about 15 percent in manufacturing. About 6 percent works at farming, forestry, mining, and fishing. This does not mean that these are unimportant occupations. Canadians have built their wealth by using their resources and by the sale of resources to the world. Trade is the lifeblood of the nation. Seventy percent of this trade is with the United States.

MINING

Minerals are the fourth largest export of Canada by value. Canada leads the world in the production of nickel and zinc. It is second in the production of asbestos, gypsum, and potash, and is a leading producer of gold, platinum, copper, lead, silver, and iron ore. Coal, gas, and oil are also important.

Although the Canadian Shield is a barrier to settlement and of little use for farming, it is a storehouse of minerals. It has yielded the world's largest nickel reserve near Sudbury, as well as copper, lead, zinc, gold, silver, iron, cobalt, platinum, magnesium, titanium, and uranium. Many mines are distant from populated areas. This means that roads or railways have had to be built across miles of forests and muskeg, or boglands, to reach them. A railway map of Canada shows single lines snaking to the north. They service such places as the nickel mine at Thompson, Manitoba, and the gold mines at Timmins. These lines carry ore concentrates to the smelters in the south or to ports for export.

What happens when the ore is used up, the price of the metals falls, or the customer does not want to buy any more? The mine cuts production or closes down and the people in the mining town must move elsewhere to find work. This is the fate of any mining town on the shield that depends solely on a mine for work. In the 1980s, the town of Schefferville, once a prosperous and thriving settlement, was closed down when the company mining the ore decided to close operations.

The shield is not the only area that is rich in minerals. The mountains of the Western Cordillera have rich deposits of coal and several ores. The discovery of gold in these mountains, ten years after the California gold rush of 1849, led to early settlement by Europeans in the area. Since then, lead, zinc, silver, and coal mines have been opened. Japan is a market for the minerals from this area. Docking facilities on the West Coast have been opened at Vancouver and Prince Rupert to send coal to Japan.

Oil refinery in Edmonton

Under the plains of the interior lie huge deposits of oil. The largest reserve is in the oil sands of Alberta, where millions of barrels—as much as the reserves of Saudi Arabia, according to some estimates—are mixed with sand close to the surface. A few plants have been opened to extract oil from these sands, but at present most of the oil comes from conventional oil wells. Coal and potash, which is used for fertilizer, are also mined.

Modern mining methods mean that these operations do not employ many people. Every miner, however, creates work for many other people—in transportation, processing, selling, and machine manufacture. The standard of living of many other Canadians depends on the state of the mining industry.

FORESTRY

Almost half of Canada's huge land area is covered by forests. Before the forests of the South were cleared, the only areas not covered by trees were the drier areas of the interior plains and the

Left: Cutting down a balsam fir   Right: Rolls of paper at a paper plant

northern areas where the growing season was too short to support forests. Trees were the first resource exploited by the settlers of the South. They were used to construct housing, barns, and furnishings, they were burned for potash, and they were made into squared timbers for export to Britain.

Today, Canada is the foremost supplier of pulp and paper in the world. The newspapers you read once may have been trees that grew in Canada. Forest products make up Canada's largest single export, and the United States is the largest single customer, taking over 60 percent of the exports. Although less than 1 percent of the labor force works in the forest, almost 8 percent depend on the forest industry. Like the mining industry, the forest industries provide thousands of jobs for others dependent on their products.

The forests of the West Coast supply over 40 percent of the lumber. A mild marine climate results in the growth of huge trees which provide excellent lumber. One Douglas fir, for example, provides enough lumber to frame five bungalows. The

A sawmill in British Columbia

forests of central and eastern Canada are mainly used for pulp and paper, although there are also sawmills. The pulp and paper mills are located in the shield area and on the coastal areas of the Atlantic region, where logs can be floated to the processing plants.

The forests of the east are threatened today by acid rain, much of which comes from the coal-burning plants in the industrial heartland of the United States. The westerly winds carry pollution over the forests of eastern Canada. Many of the lakes of the shield are crystal clear—all plant and animal life has died. The forests are beginning to show signs of damage, too. Canadians are very concerned about the lack of action by the polluters and the United States government in solving the problem of acid rain.

FARMING

Less than 5 percent of Canada is farmland, yet grains and, in particular, wheat, are a chief export. Canada is known as one of

Livestock farmers raise hogs, cattle, and chickens.

the chief wheat exporters in the world. This crop is grown on the prairies on large farms using huge machines. But this is not the only type of farming. Livestock farming, with dairy and beef cattle, hogs, and chickens, is important. Fruit and vegetables are grown in the mild valleys of British Columbia, in southern Ontario and the St. Lawrence valley, and in the fertile valleys of the East Coast.

The number of farmers is steadily decreasing. One reason is that farms are becoming larger and more mechanized. Fewer people are needed to run the farms. At the same time, the farmers' output is increasing.

Much of the best farmland in the East surrounds the cities. As these urban centers grow, the fertile land is covered with houses, roads, offices, parking lots, and factories. Studies in the 1980s showed that twenty-five acres (ten hectares) of prime farmland were being lost each day in southern Ontario alone. Canadian

Cod fishermen in Newfoundland and workers in Vancouver preparing salmon for canning

farmers produce more than enough for the present population, but there is concern that some of the best lands are being lost forever.

FISHING

Fishing is Canada's oldest export industry. The first Europeans to reach the East Coast fished for cod on the rich banks off the island of Newfoundland and took their catches back to England, Portugal, and France. Today, fishing is still a major source of work and income for the people on the East Coast. Fishing, especially for salmon, is also important on the West Coast. There are canning and freezing factories for processing in both areas. Overfishing by foreign fleets with large factory ships has reduced the stocks of fish on both coasts, and a once-important industry is in a state of crisis.

Left: Packaging refined sugar   Right: A steel mill worker

MANUFACTURING

About 15 percent of Canadians work in manufacturing
industries. Most of these industries are located in the major cities,
especially cities in Ontario and Quebec. The main industrial area
is close to the industrial area of the United States around the Great
Lakes. Many of the factories are branch plants of American firms.
One of the main industries is automobile manufacturing, and all
of the major American car firms have plants in Canada.

Steel mills line the waterfront of the city of Hamilton; textiles
are important in Quebec; and Toronto and Montreal have
hundreds of plants processing foods, making appliances, clothing,
books, and hundreds of other consumer items. In the West,
Vancouver and Edmonton are the major manufacturing cities.
Halifax, Saint John, and Moncton are the major centers in the
Maritime area.

Canada has abundant power resources on which to base
manufacturing. The oil and gas resources of western Canada are

Niagara Falls

piped to Ontario and Quebec. Huge quantities of electricity are generated from power plants on the Canadian Shield, particularly on rivers flowing into James Bay, on the Churchill River, and on several rivers flowing into the St. Lawrence. Some of this power is sent south to New England in the United States. Electricity in southern Ontario is provided by power plants at Niagara Falls and thermal power stations. The province of Quebec leads in the amount of hydroelectricity generated, with almost three times as much as the second province, British Columbia. Only Prince Edward Island does not have a major hydro development. Gas is exported to the United States from the West, as well as electricity from Quebec and Ontario.

Canadians use huge quantities of power. They are the largest users of electricity per person in the world. This is partly because some of the industries, such as aluminum smelting, use so much power.

SERVICES

As in all industrialized countries, most of the labor force works in service industries. The range of services is very great, including jobs in offices, health services, education, government, communications, and personal services such as hairdressing. The largest category is community, social and personal services.

Finance, insurance, and real estate form the second most important service industry in terms of gross domestic product. Toronto and Montreal are the leading Canadian financial centers.

Canada is so huge with so few people that transportation and communication are important in tying the country together. It was the first country to launch a domestic communications satellite and is at the forefront in developing communications technology. Thousands work in communications-related jobs such as radio, publishing, and telecommunications. Transportation is vital. Road systems in populated areas are well maintained winter and summer. Trans-Canada Highway, almost five thousand miles (eight thousand kilometers) long, links St. John's, Newfoundland to Vancouver, British Columbia. The rail system is essential to moving goods, and air transport to isolated areas.

CANADA AND THE UNITED STATES

United States President John F. Kennedy said of Canada, "Geography has made us neighbors. History has made us friends. Economics has made us partners." For Canada, the economic relationship with the United States is very important. Canada is a trading nation, and by far its most important trading partner is the United States. About two-thirds of Canada's importing and

Left: Rogers' Pass in British Columbia, discovered by a surveyor working during the construction of the railway in 1881, is in Glacier National Park, on the Trans-Canada Highway. Right: Cabot Trail, named for the explorer John Cabot, is a beautiful drive in Nova Scotia.

exporting business is with the United States. An important trade item is cars and car parts. In 1965, Canada and the United States signed an auto pact. This agreement allows cars and car parts to cross the border duty-free. Automotive products account for over 30 percent of the trade between the United States and Canada. Because so many of the manufacturing, mining, and forestry companies are branch plants of American companies, decisions about production are often made in the United States. A slight downturn in economic conditions in the United States can mean unemployment and problems in Canada. Canadians are aware that the partnership is not one of equals.

Above: Locks in the Rideau Canal raise boats in the Ottawa River.
Below: A rural schoolhouse, built in 1905, in Kemptville, Ontario

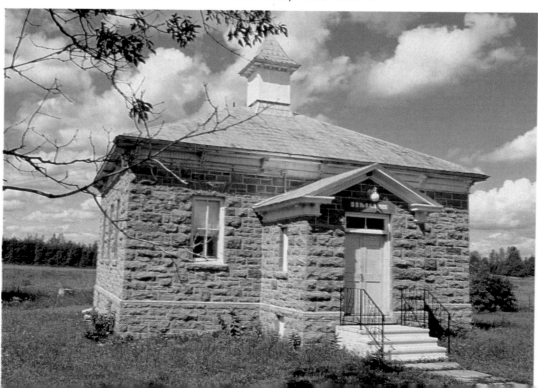

Chapter 8

COMMUNITIES

IN CANADA

In the 1920s, half the Canadian people lived in rural settlements, in small communities, or on farms. Today about 75 percent of Canadians live in urban settlements. Three cities — Toronto, Montreal, and Vancouver — house nearly 30 percent of the urban population. Life in the small communities has changed, too. Better roads, telephones, and television make them less isolated. One-room schools have disappeared and services such as medical care are more accessible. In many cases, the lack of work for young people has meant that rural settlements have stopped growing or have declined as families moved to the cities for work.

Many buildings in newer sections of communities across Canada look much the same from one settlement to another. One reason for this is that modern architectural styles, such as glass-covered skyscrapers, have become popular on a worldwide scale. In the older sections of large and small Canadian communities, the buildings that have survived reflect the history and sometimes the origins of the early settlers. These buildings have different styles in each region of Canada. Villages in eastern Ontario near the St. Lawrence River, for example, have many cut limestone houses built by the stonemasons who settled in Canada after they had finished their work on the Rideau Canal in 1832. In the

A limestone farmhouse from 1790

Maritimes, the older homes were usually built of wood, and reflected the style of housing that the settlers knew. Loyalists, for example, built homes similar to those they had left in the Thirteen Colonies.

There has been a strong movement in Canada by the federal, provincial, and local governments to preserve and restore these historic buildings. Some of the newer buildings, including housing, have been designed to blend with these older structures. This means that the distinctive regional flavor of communities, both large and small, is being actively preserved.

TORONTO

The largest and fastest growing city in Canada is Toronto. The settlement was founded in 1792 on the shores of Lake Ontario by the first governor of the area, and was known as York. It was the capital of the colony of Upper Canada and, later, of Ontario. As Ontario prospered, Toronto grew. It had a sheltered harbor that

Visitors to Toronto can go to the Space Deck near the top of the CN (Canadian National) Tower for a breathtaking view. In the foreground are Toronto Islands, mainly parkland.

from the earliest days was used as a port. The port made it a trade center; with the improvement of transportation by road and rail, it became the chief industrial center in Ontario, and later in Canada. Among the leading industries are the manufacture of machinery and electrical equipment, transportation equipment, wood, furniture and fixtures, printing and publishing, rubber and plastic products, food and beverages, metal and metal fabricating, and clothing. The city is also the financial capital of Canada.

Toronto is an interesting mix of ethnic neighborhoods. Some downtown areas have Victorian houses nestled alongside high-rise office towers. Under these office towers are shopping malls so extensive that a shopper can go from store to store without walking on the streets. The CN Tower, one of the world's tallest free-standing structures, is part of a harbor complex.

Tourists can ride glassed-in elevators up the side of the tower to view Toronto and the surrounding area from an observation deck over 1,000 feet (304 meters) high, or dine in the world's highest revolving restaurant.

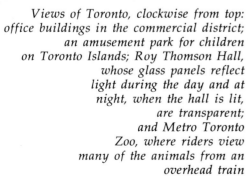

Views of Toronto, clockwise from top: office buildings in the commercial district; an amusement park for children on Toronto Islands; Roy Thomson Hall, whose glass panels reflect light during the day and at night, when the hall is lit, are transparent; and Metro Toronto Zoo, where riders view many of the animals from an overhead train

Left: City Hall and its plaza
Right: Sailing on Lake Ontario off Toronto

Another interesting building is the City Hall. An international competition was held to choose a design for the building in the 1950s. The winner from the 532 entries was a Finnish architect, Viljo Revell, whose design featured two curved towers, with the round dome of the council chambers resting between them.

Toronto is the base for the English-speaking culture in Canada. In addition to two universities, the city is home to the Royal Ontario Museum; the Ontario Art Gallery, with its collection of Henry Moore works; the innovative Ontario Science Centre, built by Japanese-Canadian architect Raymond Moriyama; the Toronto symphony orchestra; the National Ballet of Canada; and the Canadian Opera Company.

MONTREAL

Montreal, the second-largest city in Canada, is situated on an island in the St. Lawrence River, where rapids at one time made it impossible for oceangoing ships to sail any farther upstream into the Great Lakes. The most important tributary of the St. Lawrence, the Ottawa River, which provided a route to the west for the fur traders, joins the main stream at this point. This location made the city a natural trade center. Today, Montreal is a major industrial, commercial, financial, and transportation center, and the largest French-speaking city outside Paris.

Montreal was founded in 1642. It was the center of the fur trade and the port from which the voyageurs set out along the Ottawa River to trade in the interior. Explorers from Montreal traveled down the Mississippi, into the American west, and north to the Athabasca River.

Early in the nineteenth century, Montreal grew rapidly as the agricultural land around the city was settled. With the construction of the Lachine Canal, which made transportation into the Great Lakes possible, and railways, Montreal became the leading port and industrial center in Canada. Its products include food and beverages, clothing, metal products, transportation equipment, and chemical products. Although Vancouver now handles a much larger tonnage of goods, Montreal is still the main port of the eastern seaboard.

Montreal is the center for French-speaking culture in Canada. The Quebec National Library, which has copies of all works published in the province since the library's founding, is located in the city. There are numerous theater groups and a center for the performing arts at Place des Arts. Two of the main French-

Top: The Lachine Canal
in Montreal is no longer
used for shipping and
the area is being
converted into a recreational area.
Middle: Downtown Montreal
Bottom: Although Montreal
is 1,000 miles (1,609
kilometers) from the ocean,
it is a major port.

Above: Colorful old homes and sidewalk cafes in Place Jacques Cartier are part of the charm of Montreal. Below: Habitat was built for Expo 67. Each block is a self-contained living unit.

Jacques Cartier Bridge connects Montreal with Ile Ste-Helene.

language newspapers in Canada are published here. There are four universities, two of which are French-speaking. About two-thirds of the population is French Canadian.

Many old buildings in Montreal were cleared in the 1960s to make way for the skyscrapers that now mark the skyline. Place Ville-Marie is the most famous of these. The old town, near the port, has been restored and renovated to provide a lively social center. In 1967, the city was host to the world for Expo 67, a very successful fair that marked Canada's centennial. The grounds for the fair are now the site of an annual exhibition. The Olympic Stadium was built to host the 1976 Olympic Games.

VANCOUVER

Canada's third-largest city, Vancouver, British Columbia, has a beautiful location. The city lies on a peninsula at the mouth of the

Vancouver is the commercial, financial, and industrial center of British Columbia.

Fraser River and is washed by the salt waters of the Strait of Georgia. The snowcapped peaks of the majestic Coastal Ranges are the backdrop.

The city was founded in 1885 when the Canadian Pacific Railway transcontinental terminal was built on the peninsula. The deep, sheltered harbor was a natural advantage. The city grew very rapidly, and by the 1920s was already Canada's third-largest city. Vancouver handles wheat and other grains, and lumber, potash, and coal for export to the Pacific Rim countries, particularly Japan. It is an important industrial center, with wood, furniture, paper, publishing, food, and beverage industries, machinery and transportation equipment manufacturing, and metal fabricating.

Top: Vancouver, with Vancouver Island
in the background Below: The annual sea
festival in English Bay, and Gastown,
a restored nineteenth-century
area with some modern construction

Coal Harbour, with private boats, and Chinatown in Vancouver

The city is also a financial center for the West. The Bank of British Columbia; MacMillan Bloedel, a major lumber company; Cominco, a mining company; and Canadian Pacific Air all have head offices here.

Vancouver is a city that offers outdoor recreation for its inhabitants. They can ski in the mountains, sail or bathe in the nearby ocean, or simply enjoy one of the city's many parks, of which Stanley Park is the most famous. This park, with a beautiful location on a peninsula, was set aside for public use when the city was founded.

In 1986, the city was host to Expo 86, which attracted millions of visitors from around the world. The Chinatown area of Vancouver is another tourist attraction. The city has an active cultural life, with its own symphony orchestra, art gallery, museums, an opera association, and two universities.

Rideau Falls, with Ottawa City Hall on the right

OTTAWA

Ottawa is the capital of Canada and, together with Hull across the Ottawa River, is the fourth-largest urban center. Queen Victoria chose Ottawa, then a lumber town called Bytown, as the capital of the province of Canada in 1857. In 1867, at the time of Confederation, Ottawa was chosen as the national capital. The largest number of workers in the city are in government service. The second-largest industry is tourism.

Ottawa is a beautiful city. The banks of the Ottawa River and

Tulips in bloom and an outdoor chess board

roadways through the city are lined with parks. In spring, the parks blossom with thousands of tulips donated by The Netherlands in gratitude for hospitality given their queen during World War II. Railways have been removed from the core and the Rideau Canal, which was built between 1826 and 1832 to link the Ottawa River and Lake Ontario, is used for skating in winter. The Rideau Centre, a downtown convention, shopping, and hotel complex, was opened in 1983. Tourists can spend days visiting the many interesting buildings, such as the Parliament buildings, the National Arts Centre, the national museums, and the National Gallery.

Winter in Major's Hill Park (above), with the Chateau Laurier
Hotel in the background and an old fish market in the Byward
Market area (below), which has existed in Ottawa since 1846.

The Muttart Conservatory and, in the background across the Saskatchewan River, the Edmonton skyline

EDMONTON

Edmonton, the capital of Alberta and the largest city on the prairies, is located on the banks of the North Saskatchewan River. It has been given the name "Gateway to the North," as the road, rail, and air routes into the Mackenzie River valley and the North pass through. Edmonton was founded in the days of the fur trade, but it did not start to grow until it was reached by the railway, when settlement of the surrounding agricultural lands began.

The discovery of oil nearby in 1947 gave Edmonton a huge boost. Today it has oil refineries and food processing industries. A large number of people work in government services, and Edmonton is a major commercial center.

Jasper Avenue (above) and Diamond Park (below) in Edmonton

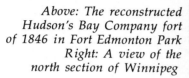

Above: The reconstructed Hudson's Bay Company fort of 1846 in Fort Edmonton Park Right: A view of the north section of Winnipeg

With its recent growth, Edmonton is a very modern city. A new convention center has been built in a series of terraces into the riverbank, which is bordered by parks, golf courses, and woodland trails. The Muttart Conservatory, Citadel Theatre, Provincial Museum, Strathcona Science Park, Space Science Centre, and reconstructed Fort Edmonton are also popular attractions. In recognition of the numerous groups who have settled the area, the city holds a week-long Heritage Festival each year to celebrate its history.

WINNIPEG

Winnipeg is the capital of Manitoba. It grew up at the place known as the Forks, where the Red River is joined by the Assiniboine River. French and British traders built fur posts at this

Views of Winnipeg, clockwise from top left: weekend market in Old Market Square, a branch of the Royal Canadian Mint, the Legislative building, and Assiniboine Park

site and it was the center of the Red River settlement, the first agricultural settlement by Europeans in the west. Today Winnipeg is often called the "Gateway to the West," as it is the focus of transportation routes onto the prairies. It lies only sixty miles (ninety-seven kilometers) north of the United States border, hedged in by the Canadian Shield to the east and Lake Winnipeg to the north.

The building of the railways caused Winnipeg's growth. Wheat producers from the prairies sent their grain through the city

The Assiniboine River meets the Red River at downtown Winnipeg.

eastwards through the Great Lakes for export. Winnipeg today has industries largely based on its role as a transportation center, as well as flour mills and meat packing plants.

A disastrous flood of the Red River in 1950 damaged many of the buildings, and since the 1960s many new buildings have been added. A new city hall was built, as well as the planetarium, the Manitoba Museum of Man and Nature, and a concert hall. The annual Manitoba Music Festival is the largest music festival in Canada. Another major attraction nearby is Lower Fort Garry, a historic reconstruction of the Hudson's Bay Company depot on the Red River.

The Chateau Frontenac Hotel, built in 1893, stands above the Lower Town in Quebec City.

QUEBEC CITY

Quebec City is the capital of the province of Quebec, the oldest city in Canada. It is a French-speaking city, the cradle of French civilization in North America, and has few English-speaking Canadians. It is located on the north shore of the St. Lawrence, where the river becomes less than a mile wide. The town was built on a headland about three hundred feet (ninety-one meters) high that was easily defended. In its history, the people of the city beat off attacks by the British and Americans. Quebec City was a leading port for centuries, as it was difficult for sailing ships to navigate upstream on the St. Lawrence. As soon as steamships were able to reach upriver to Montreal, Quebec City lost its leading position.

Some scenes of Quebec City
are an outdoor cafe (top),
the Citadel (above), and Rue St. Louis
(left) in the old city.

Part of the Winter Carnival celebration (left) and the Seminary, Canada's oldest institute of higher learning, from Rue St. Andre in the Lower Town (right)

The city was built on two levels—the Lower Town at the foot of the headland, and the Upper Town on the heights. A fort, called the Citadel, and a defensive wall were built on the headland to protect the Upper Town. Within the walls were the government buildings and churches. Today, Quebec is the only walled city in North America.

The Lower Town was the residential and commercial part of the city. The historical buildings of this old city have been restored and maintained. Tourists to the city visit the fortifications, the Plains of Abraham (where the British and French forces met in 1759 in the decisive battle for the city), Place Royale, a partial reconstruction of the old city, the Old Port, churches, and museums.

Most people work in government, administration, or tourist services. A major attraction each winter is the Winter Carnival. A festival is held each July.

Soldiers (left), stationed at the fortress at Louisbourg, guarded the entrance to the St. Lawrence River. The site, including the Governor's Apartment (right), has been restored.

HALIFAX

Halifax, the capital city of Nova Scotia, and the largest city in the Maritime provinces, has one of the world's largest harbors. The city is built on a peninsula that separates two bodies of water, the Bedford Basin and Halifax Harbour. On the east side of the harbor, opposite Halifax, is the city of Dartmouth, also a port and industrial center.

The harbor has always been important to Halifax. When the city was founded in 1749, the British government was worried that the great French fortress at Louisbourg on Cape Breton Island would be used as a base to attack the British colonies. One of the chief landmarks in Halifax today is the Citadel, a fortification that sits high on the hill that overlooks the great harbor. The present Citadel was built between 1828 to 1856—the fourth fort to be built on the site.

The restored waterfront of Halifax

The city is sometimes called the "Warden of the North" because of its strategic location close to the main Atlantic shipping route. This location and its ice-free and easily defended harbor made Halifax particularly important during World War I and World War II. From 1939 to 1945 it was the chief port sending supplies across the Atlantic to Allied forces. The city was struck by tragedy during World War I. Early on a December morning in 1917, a Belgian ship collided with a French vessel carrying explosives and arms. The French ship was blown a mile high, and the area was rocked by an explosion so great that it was heard in Prince Edward Island and broke windows in homes 100 miles (161 kilometers) away. The industrial area of the city was leveled, and tidal waves and fires caused more destruction. Over sixteen hundred people died, and millions of dollars worth of damage was done. Relief help poured in from the rest of Canada and from the United States.

The port of Halifax is especially busy in winter when the St. Lawrence Seaway is closed.

Today, Halifax is Canada's largest ice-free port on the eastern coast. It is still an important naval and military base. The port facilities are modern and can handle the largest ships built. Containers can be unloaded and shipped by rail to central Canada when the St. Lawrence Seaway is closed. Because of the port functions, industries have grown up around the harbor.

The city was one of the first in Canada to redevelop its downtown area. The old waterfront area has been restored, with stores and cultural facilities. Across the harbor, the historic center of Dartmouth was restored also. Halifax is the cultural center of Nova Scotia, with universities, theater, a literary tradition that includes the publication of the first newspaper in Canada, museums, and archives.

A rural area in the province of Quebec

VILLAGES IN QUEBEC

The rural villages in the farming areas of the province of Quebec have a settlement pattern that is quite distinct. They usually have a row of houses along the main road, with a Catholic church, school, and main services in a central area. In these villages, the people are usually all French-speaking. The houses are often old and based on traditional architecture, with steep sloping roofs and dormer windows. The early settlers needed the rivers for transportation, so they built their homes close to the riverbanks. Each settler had a long narrow lot of land stretching back from the river for about one mile. Today this long lot pattern, which dates from the seventeenth century, is still clearly visible in the province of Quebec.

*Airplanes (left) are an important means of transportation in the North and the
Dempster Highway (right) links Inuvik to Dawson in the Yukon Territory.*

INUVIK—A NORTHERN COMMUNITY

Inuvik is the largest community in Canada north of the Arctic
Circle. About three thousand people, Inuit, Indians, and whites,
live in this modern settlement located at the delta of the
Mackenzie River. Compared with communities in the South,
Inuvik is isolated, but not when compared with some other
communities of the North. It can be reached by barges along the
Mackenzie River in summer. In winter, the river freezes and can
be used as a road. The Dempster Highway links the settlement to
Dawson in the Yukon Territory. Like all northern communities,
the most important transportation link for people is the airplane.

Living so far north can present problems. Inuvik lies in the land
of the midnight sun, where in summer the sun does not set for
one month; in winter, there is darkness for one month. The

Left: Homes in Inuvik Right: An Inuit child

ground is permanently frozen, and special types of houses have to be designed. The bases of the houses have to be separated from the ground by insulation so they do not sink into the permafrost as they are heated. Roads and airstrips have to be specially constructed so they do not sink into the top layer when it thaws in the brief summer.

The community is the center for oil-drilling activities in the Beaufort Sea. There are buildings that are found in many small communities, such as a bank, stores, and a firehouse. There are residential halls for children who come to the high school from communities as far as 700 miles (1,127 kilometers) away. These children come from other Arctic communities that are so small that they can provide only primary education. For them, Inuvik, with its hotels for visitors, hospital, and large government buildings, must seem like a large Canadian city!

The Parliament buildings overlook a harbor in James Bay, Victoria, British Columbia (above);
a typical residential house in Fredericton, New Brunswick (below left);
and a woman filleting an Arctic char in the Northwest Territories (below right)

Chapter 9

LIVING IN CANADA

The regional nature of Canada and the wide range of ethnic groups mean that there is variety in lifestyles. The Inuit families of Nain, a coastal community in Labrador, for example, spend the summer months fishing for arctic char along the coast, and do not return to their houses until the fall. A family in Victoria, British Columbia, where the climate is mild in winter, may have sailing as a year-round hobby. Unlike people in most other parts of the country, they will not spend time cleaning snow from driveways or deicing windshields in winter.

The different geographic areas and the cultural diversity of the people do not make it easy to give a general idea of everyday life for a typical family. Yet there are some features that most families have in common.

EVERYDAY LIFE IN CANADA

Most people in Canada have a lifestyle that is similar to that of people in other Western countries. They are housed in single-family homes, apartments, or condominiums. Most families own at least one car. In rural areas, cars are necessary for family

At sunrise in Montreal, the expressways are not yet busy.

shopping and for travel to work. Although larger cities and towns have public transportation, such as buses, cars are still the most common form of transportation. Most homes have at least one telephone, which is also a necessity.

In many families, both parents work at full-time or part-time jobs. Expressways in the larger cities are already crowded by 7:00 in the morning with people on their way to work. School usually starts at 9:00 in the morning, and lasts until 3:00 in the afternoon. Where schools are within walking distance, students return home for lunch. In rural areas, they spend all day at school. They are picked up by school buses in the morning, eat a packed lunch at school, and return home by school bus.

This daily routine makes it difficult for the first two meals of the day, breakfast and lunch, to be family meals. The evening meal, which is usually the largest meal of the day, is the most common time for the family to sit together. The most popular pastime in the evening is watching television.

Christmas decorations at Robson Square in Vancouver, British Columbia

Weekends are the time for recreation in Canadian families. Few stores and businesses can be legally open in Canada on Sunday, which is officially a public holiday, so few people are at work. For many Canadians, weekends are the time for enjoying the outdoors, especially in summer.

NATIONAL HOLIDAYS

The most important national holiday in Canada is Canada Day, celebrated on July 1 or, if this date falls on a Sunday, on July 2. This is Canada's official "birthday." Communities organize special celebrations, often with displays of fireworks or picnics.

Victoria Day, on May 24, or the first Monday before May 25, is a celebration of the birthday of Queen Victoria. In Quebec it is called Dollard Day. Fireworks are let off after dusk, and even if the weather is unseasonably cold, it is still regarded as the first holiday weekend of the summer season. Labour Day, the first Monday in September, marks the end of the summer season for many families as schools open on the following day.

Thanksgiving, with a traditional stuffed turkey and pumpkin pie, is celebrated on the second Monday in October. Christmas Day, Boxing Day (December 26), and New Year's Day are also public holidays, although many stores are opened on Boxing Day. In the Christmas season, families celebrate according to their traditional customs and prepare traditional foods. Good Friday and Easter Monday mark the Easter season. Chocolate eggs and Easter bunnies are sold in the stores, and many parents hide candies for children to find on Easter Sunday.

SPORTS AND RECREATION

A survey of the recreational equipment owned by Canadians shows the same main categories as their clothing: winter equipment and summer equipment. A growing number of families own cross-country skis and downhill skis. Over 10 percent have snowmobiles. It would be difficult to find a family that does not own a pair of hockey or figure skates. Over half of the households surveyed owned bicycles, and overnight camping equipment, such as tents and tent trailers, were common. In Alberta alone, over 40 percent of families were equipped for camping.

There is one sport above others for which Canada and Canadians are known—ice hockey. Ice hockey was first played in Canada in 1875, and became popular so quickly that in less than ten years there was an amateur national association. Most communities have local arenas with ice rinks and organized clubs for youngsters to learn the game. Any patch of ice large enough to

*Snowmobiling (above) and ice hockey (below) are popular sports,
but ice hockey is the favorite—for players and spectators alike.*

Skating on the Rideau Canal in Ottawa

hold a net and a few players is used for practice outside of school. The televised National Hockey League games between the major teams are watched by thousands across the country, and the results are analyzed at length in newspapers and by the fans.

Local ice rinks are used also for curling, a traditional Scottish game that Canadians have adopted, and for figure skating. Canada has produced a number of world champions in figure skating, and the sport shows no sign of decreasing in popularity.

In the summer months, Canadians take to the outdoors. There are also hundreds of parks that can be used for camping, hiking, and swimming. Canada's national parks are administered by the federal government. In area, Canada has the largest national park system in the world. There are national parks in every province, and about twenty million visits are recorded each year. There are also provincial and local parks that can be used for outdoor activities, such as picnics, swimming, boating, hiking, cycling, walking, or simply relaxing. Canadians are conscious of the need to care for their environment, and the parks are well maintained.

Above: A ski slope in Mount Royal Park in Montreal   Below: In British Columbia, the mountains (left) and Takakkaw Falls (right) are popular vacation spots.

Maligne Lake in Jasper National Park, Alberta

Many Canadians enjoy hunting as a sport. This activity is carefully controlled by government regulations. Hunters must have licenses to kill animals and permits to own and use guns. The most common large-game animals taken are white-tailed deer and moose. Birds, particularly ducks, grouse, and geese, also are killed in large numbers. Opportunities for hunting in Canada are so attractive that tourists from all over the world come to enjoy the sport.

With thousands of lakes dotting the land, it is no surprise that fishing is also a popular pastime, even in winter. For ice fishing, a hole is cut through the ice, and lines with lures attached are lowered into the water. Some lakes are dotted in winter with ice huts used by the patient fishermen.

The Arts Building of McGill University, Montreal

EDUCATION

Since 1867, the education of the population is the responsibility of the provinces. Each province has a department of education that decides what will be taught in the schools and teacher qualifications. School districts are run by local or regional boards of elected trustees, who choose administrators for the school systems. The public school system provides for free education, from enrollment until graduation.

In most provinces, children start school at six years of age and must stay until they are sixteen years old. There are two main stages of schooling—primary education and secondary education. In some provinces, there are some intermediary schools called junior high schools that teach students between the ages of twelve

119

The University of Winnipeg

and fifteen. Secondary schools in most provinces provide four years of schooling.

Students who want to continue their education after secondary school can attend community colleges, which often include work-related skills in their courses, or one of the many universities, which provide academic courses. Students whose parents are unable to afford the fees required can apply for financial assistance from the government.

SOCIAL SERVICES

The humiliating effects of the Great Depression on the lives of hardworking and proud, independent Canadians changed Canada. Since then, the federal and provincial governments have set up programs to provide a minimum standard of care for people.

Governments now provide social services for Canadians from the time of their birth to old age. Health care is universal and includes payment of doctors' fees and hospital costs. Each month, families receive an allowance from the government for children under the age of eighteen.

Workers also are protected if they lose their jobs. Unemployment insurance provides an income after twenty weeks of full-time work. Injured workers are covered under workers' compensation schemes administered by provincial governments.

At retirement, Canadians are eligible to receive old age security benefits. In addition, they may receive pensions from the Canada Pension Plan or the Quebec Pension Plan, as well as income supplements.

These measures provide some security to Canadians who, through no fault of their own, find themselves out of work or unable to make a living. There is an awareness that more needs to be done to help the disadvantaged, and programs are under constant review.

FOOD

If you asked Canadians to name some national foods, you would probably be faced with a long, thoughtful pause. So many different recipes originated in other lands and were adapted to life in Canada that it is difficult to think of national dishes. One might be French-Canadian pea soup, a delicious adaptation of the traditional food carried by the voyageurs on their long trips. Dried peas are simmered in water with a ham bone, chopped onion, and seasoning until a thick, wholesome soup is produced. Another is

Above: Preparing lobster dinners on Prince Edward Island
Below: Greek food being cooked for an ethnic festival in Vancouver

maple syrup, made from the sap of the maple tree, and boiled, preferably over a wood fire, until it thickens.

The real joy of food in Canada is that there is such a variety. Small stores and supermarkets stock foods that are made in Canada but have their origins in other lands, as well as imported specialities. These can range from German-style breads to Chinese cabbage or English mincemeat. These are all supplemented by the delicious specialities of each region, from seafoods on the East and West coasts, to the tender beef of Alberta.

CANADIAN CULTURE

In the 1980s, the Canadian Radio-television and Telecommunications Commission (CRTC), a body of the Canadian government that regulates the broadcasting system, ruled that a certain amount of Canadian music was to be played on radio stations, and specified the amount of Canadian content on TV stations. These rules were an attempt to have Canadian voices heard among the masses of popular entertainment being broadcast across the border from the United States. The cultural messages that come from the United States are certainly strong — movies, books, magazines, TV programs, fads, and fashions — but the Canadian experience has given rise to a distinct Canadian voice, which has found expression in films, plays, dance, literature, and the work of artists.

Like its people, Canadian culture is diverse. As an example, each region has distinctive literature. Several Canadian writers have produced works that are known worldwide, and that depict the Canadian experience. Lucy Maud Montgomery's books, especially the series about Anne of Green Gables, are so popular

A basketweaver (top right), an Inuit carving (bottom right) of an ivory polar bear on a soapstone rock, and an Inuit sculpture (left) called the Tree of Life

that Green Gables on Prince Edward Island is visited by people from around the world. Mordecai Richler, Hugh McLennan, Robertson Davies, Margaret Laurence, Anne Hebert, Antonine Maillet, Gabrielle Roy, Michel Tremblay, Farley Mowat, and Margaret Atwood are among contemporary writers whose works have an audience beyond Canada.

The art of Inuit printmakers and sculptors, such as Pitseolak and Makpaaq, is prized by collectors. The works show the legends, mythologies, and way of life of the people, as well as the animals, fish, and birds of the North. Norval Morrisseau and Daphne Odjig are both Native artists whose paintings interpret the legends and experience of their people. Both have exhibited internationally. Their success and recognition have encouraged other Native artists to express their talents.

Icebergs, Davis Strait *by Lawren Harris, one of the Group of Seven*

The birth of a distinctive non-Native Canadian style of painting is traced to the Group of Seven. These men broke away from the traditional Victorian style of realism to paint the Canadian wilderness as they saw it. They are recognized as the founders of a truly national form of painting.

Each region of Canada has produced renowned artists who have interpreted their environment in their own unique way. Alexander Colville, an East Coast artist, produces hauntingly realistic paintings that always leave the viewer with a feeling of imminent danger even though the subject matter may be as simple as the portrait of a hunting dog on the trail. Many of the landscape paintings of Quebec artist Jean-Paul Lemieux are dominated by a distant flat horizon and seemingly isolated figures. William Kurelek, a Canadian of Ukrainian descent, painted the prairies and the childhood he knew in a series that has been published in books for children, *A Prairie Boy's Winter*, *Lumberjack*, and *A Prairie Boy's Summer*.

In music, pianist Glenn Gould is remembered for his interpretations of Johann Sebastian Bach's works, and Maureen Forrester and Jon Vickers are internationally known singers. There is a thriving theatrical community in Canada that includes dance companies and drama groups. Many of these groups receive financial assistance from cultural agencies such as the Canada Council. In order to be viable, most of these companies need to tour the country, which exposes them to a wide audience.

In film, the National Film Board (NFB), established by the federal government in 1939, has won hundreds of international awards. The film board largely makes documentary and animation films. Canada is a world leader in film animation, largely as a result of the work of the NFB. The film board also proved to be the training ground for several filmmakers, such as Denys Arcand, who have since made successful commercial films. The film industry in Canada, which has only survived with help from the federal government, always has to compete with American movies at the box office.

The federal government has taken an active role in nurturing cultural activities of all kinds in Canada, largely by providing financial assistance. There have been times when it seemed as though cultural pressures from the United States were too strong to resist, and Canada was just an extension of the United States. This government assistance has heightened Canadians' awareness of their past and their distinctiveness as a people.

Above: The city of St. John's, Newfoundland, is built on steep, rocky slopes.
Below: Waterton Lakes National Park in Alberta

MAP KEY

Statute Miles

100   0   100   200   300

Lambert Conformal Conic Projection

Same Scale as Main Map

GENERAL INFORMATION

Official Name: Canada

Capital: Ottawa

Official Languages: English; French. Canada is officially a bilingual country. One-third of the people speak French. The largest French-speaking population is in the province of Quebec.

Government: Canada is a constitutional monarchy with a parliamentary system of government. It is a federal state. Queen Elizabeth is the official head of state. But in practice Canada is governed by the prime minister, usually the leader of the party with the most seats in the House of Commons, the dominant chamber of the bicameral Parliament. The upper house of Parliament is the Senate.
   Executive power is vested in the governor-general, but this is exercised through a prime minister and his/her cabinet. The cabinet is chosen by the prime minster from members of his/her party holding seats in the House of Commons.
   Each of the ten provinces has a lieutenant governor and its own unicameral legislature.

National Anthem: "O Canada," approved in 1976, and officially made the national anthem in 1980. The music was composed by Calixa Lavallee.

Flag: The flag is red, with a white square the width of the flag in the center bearing a single red maple leaf. The flag was adopted in 1965.

Money: The basic monetary unit is the Canadian dollar. In January 1996, the Canadian dollar was worth $0.74 in United States currency.

Weights and Measures: By 1985 Canada's conversion to the metric system was all but complete.

Population: 27,896,859, 1991 census; 29,107,000, 1994 estimate. In 1993, 23 percent of the population was rural and 77 percent urban. The density (8 per square mile, 3 per square kilometer) is among the lowest in the world. Most of the population is clustered within 100 miles (160 kilometers) of the United States border.

Major Cities (Metropolitan areas):
   (Population figures based on 1991 census)

Toronto 3,893,046	Calgary 754,033
Montreal 3,127,242	Winnipeg 652,354
Vancouver 1,602,502	Quebec City 645,550
Ottawa 920,857	Hamilton 599,760
Edmonton 839,924	

Religion: Canadians have religious freedom. Ninety percent of the population are Christians with 47 percent of those Roman Catholic, and the rest United Church, Anglican, Presbyterian, Baptist, and Lutheran. The remaining 10 percent embrace Judaism, Buddhism, Sikhism, Hinduism, Islam, the Baha'i Faith, or native religions.

GEOGRAPHY

Highest Point: Mt. Logan, 19,524 ft. (5,951 m), in the St. Elian Mountains of the Yukon Territory

Lowest Point: Sea level

Coastline: 151,488 mi. (243,797 km). The coastline borders three oceans: the North Pacific on the west, the North Atlantic on the east, and the Arctic on the north

Rivers: The Mackenzie and the St. Lawrence are second and third in North America (after the Mississippi-Missouri) in the amount of water they discharge. The longest rivers are the Mackenzie (2,635 mi.; 4,241 k), Saskatchewan (1,205 mi.; 1,939 k), Churchill (1,000 mi.; 1,609 km), and Fraser (850 mi.; 1,367 km). The St. Lawrence, though not the longest river (800 mi.; 1,287 km), has a huge drainage area, part of which is in the United States. This river and its tributary, the Ottawa River (790 mi.; 1,271 km), and the Great Lakes were historic waterways into the interior of the continent.

Mountains: Sixteen percent of Canada's land area is covered by the mountains of the Western Cordillera, which have some of the highest peaks in North America. These are glaciated mountains, and some glaciers still exist. The Appalachian Mountains are lower and form about 2 percent of the land mass.

Climate: The climate of Canada is as varied as its geography. In much of the country winter lasts longer than summer, though even in the North summer can be very hot with long hours of sunlight. The central provinces receive the most snow, far more than the Arctic, which in fact receives little precipitation. The large bodies of water surrounding the continent have a moderating effect on the climate, making winters warmer and summers cooler. Terrain also plays a part. Thus the Pacific Coast is cool and fairly dry in summer; mild, cloudy, and wet in winter. Interior British Columbia is drier and much colder in winter. From the Rocky Mountains to the Great Lakes there are long, cold winters and short, warm summers, with scanty precipitation. Southern Ontario and Quebec have a humid climate, with cold winters and hot summers. The Atlantic Provinces have precipitation all year. The climate becomes progressively colder and the growing season shorter in northern latitudes. At the Arctic shores the climate is very cold in winter, with a short (2 month) summer period when the daily temperature does not average above 50° F. (10° C).

Greatest Distances: North to south—2,875 mi. (4,637 km)
East to west—3,223 mi. (5,187 km)

Area: 3,831,033 sq. mi. (9,922,330 km²)

NATURE

Trees: Forests cover about 50 percent of the Canadian land surface. The trees are mainly cone-bearing (coniferous) and include pine, spruce, hemlock, fir, cedar, juniper, cypress, and yew. Deciduous trees are found mostly in southern Ontario.

These species include maple, oak, birch, poplar, hickory, ash, and elm. The coniferous forests of the West Coast are particularly valuable for their lumber.

Fish: There are about 950 species of fish in Canadian waters. About 760 of these are seawater species. The most common are salmon, whitefish, bass, char, cod, herring, mackerel, perch, pickerel, pike, smelt, sturgeon, trout, and tuna. Two species of sea mammals — the seal and the whale — were once numerous. Because the whale has been overhunted, 4 of the 33 species are now rare — the bowhead, right whale, humpback, and blue whale.

Animals: Some animals that were very numerous before European settlement, such as the prairie bison (buffalo), were so reduced in number that they became an endangered species. The most important animals in Canada are deer (moose, caribou), wapiti (otherwise known as the American elk), bears (black, grizzly, and polar), wolves, beaver, muskrat, and foxes. Animals trapped for their fur include the following: badger, bear, beaver, bobcat, cougar, coyote, ermine, fisher, fox, lynx, marten, mink, muskrat, otter, raccoon, skunk, squirrel, and wolf. Animals kept domestically are cattle (dairy and beef), hogs, horses, sheep, goats, chickens, ducks, geese, and fur-bearing animals such as mink and fox.

Birds: Canada has many birds, but the largest number of species are in the warmer south. There are 82 bird sanctuaries as well as national and provincial parks for their protection. Common birds are gulls, doves, ducks, loons, geese, hawks, owls, partridge, grouse, ptarmigan, tern, pheasants, sea birds (cormorants, herons), and perching birds such as sparrows and finches. The passenger pigeon, once so numerous that migrating flocks darkened the sky for hours, was wiped out by hunters in the 1880s. Similarly, the great auk that once nested on islands off the East Coast, was exterminated by the mid-1800s.

EVERYDAY LIFE

Food: British Columbia is famous for its seafood, especially king crab and salmon. It also produces a great deal of fruit — peaches, cherries, grapes, etc., as well as its own wine. In the Prairies the beef is excellent. Wild rice is a great delicacy collected by a number of Indian tribes. Southern Ontario is the great fruit and vegetable area of Canada, as well as another wine producing region. Quebec has a fine culinary tradition that owes much to its French ancestry, but has developed a distinctive French-Canadian style. The Maritime Provinces are noted also for their seafood — clams, oysters, salmon, lobster, snow crab, cod, markeral, herring, and scallops. In Newfoundland cod is a staple of the diet. In the Northwest Territories moose meat and fresh lake fish are widely available.

Housing: Traditional homes in older communities reflect the styles of the country of their builders' origins, and use local building materials. In eastern Ontario, for example, cut limestone was used frequently and was worked by local stone masons. In the Maritimes, most homes are made of wood. Contemporary homes comprise a variety of styles and materials. In 1981, 46 percent of the 8,700,000 dwelling units in Canada were single-family detached; 18 percent were attached or row houses; and 36 percent were apartments. Sixty-five percent of the total were built after World War II.

National Holidays:

January 1, New Year's Day
Good Friday
Easter
Monday nearest May 24, Victoria Day (in Quebec, Dollard Day)
July 1, Canada Day
First Monday in September, Labour Day
Second Monday in October, Thanksgiving Day
December 25, Christmas Day
December 26, Boxing Day

Culture: Canada is a nation of immigrants. Its variety of peoples makes its cultural life rich and varied. Each region has produced a distinctive literature.

French-Canadian literature has reflected the long struggle to preserve the French cultural heritage in the New World. French-Canadian historical writing flourished in the 1840s. The *Histoire du Canada*, published by F.X. Garneau from 1845-48, was considered to be the standard history of that period. A great literary renaissance in Quebec in the wake of the Quiet Revolution produced novelists, poets, and dramatists of international reputation including Michel Tremblay, Anne Hebert, Marie-Claire Blais, and Antonine Maillet, whose words were acclaimed in France and translated into English.

English-Canadian literature began with the accounts of travelers. The first important English-Canadian novel was *Wacousta* (1832) by John Richardson, a tale of Pontiac's Indian conspiracy. Thomas Chandler Haliburton, a Nova Scotian judge, ranks as the most distinguished literary figure of the period—the creator of Sam Slick, the Yankee peddler who sold wooden clocks. Lucy Maud Montgomery's series about Anne of Green Gables, as well as the works of Mordecai Richler, Robertson Davies, Hugh McLennan, Margaret Laurence, Farley Mowat, and Margaret Atwood are known throughout the world.

The art of Inuit printmakers and sculptors is praised by collectors. The works reflect the legends and culture of the Eskimos of the north. Norval Morrisseau and Daphne Odjig are Native artists who have exhibited internationally.

Glenn Gould is Canada's best-known pianist, who specialized in the works of J.S. Bach. There is a creative and energetic theatrical community in Canada. The Shakespeare summer festival in Stratford, Ontario, is known throughout the world.

The Canadian National Film Board is best known for its documentaries and has won hundreds of international awards.

Most larger cities have orchestras (the Montreal Symphony Orchestra is the best known), theater groups, dance groups, and art galleries. The federal government has taken an active role in the support of the arts, creating regional centers for the performing arts.

Sports and Recreation: Ice hockey originated in Montreal in 1875 and gained immediate popularity. Skating has always been popular. The first covered skating rink was built in Quebec City in 1852. Most communities have an ice rink, and curling and speed and figure skating are popular forms of recreation. Lacrosse is Canada's national game. Basketball was organized by a Canadian, too. Football is also a popular team sport. Tennis and soccer have grown in popularity in recent years. Canada has a strong network of swimming clubs. Camping, hiking, and swimming are popular in summer.

Health: Canada has had a system of public health care for over 25 years. Life expectancy is 74 for men and 81 for women, one of the highest in the world.

Communication: Because of its immense size and its small population, communications are extremely important in Canada. It was the third country, after the U.S. and the U.S.S.R. to put a communications satellite into orbit. Canada now has 8 such satellites. Communications are rapidly becoming computerized. There are 20 million telephones in the country, or one for every 1.2 people. There is direct dialing to more than 180 countries. Daily newspapers number about 95 in the English language and 11 in French. *La Presse* (French) of Montreal and the *Globe and Mail* (English) of Toronto are two of Canada's largest dailies. Seventy-five ethnic weekly papers are published.

Transportation: Four-fifths of urban travel is by private car. Road transportation is vital. The Trans-Canada Highway, completed in 1962, links St. John's, Newfoundland, on the Atlantic Coast with Victoria, British Columbia, on the Pacific Coast. The Alaska Highway, 40 years old in 1982, links Dawson Creek, British Columbia, to Fairbanks, Alaska. The Klondike Highway links Skagway to Dawson, and the Dempster Highway links Dawson with Inuvik. In 1991, 53,169 mi. (85,563 km) of railway track were in operation. The largest amount of track is under the control of the government-owned Canadian National Railways. The other large holder is Canadian Pacific, a joint-stock corporation. Most rail is for moving freight. Canada has 25 deep-water ports. Vancouver is the leading port; Montreal is second. The main commercial waterway is the St. Lawrence Seaway. Vessels rise through locks on the 2,250-mi. (3,621-km) journey from the Atlantic to Lake Superior. The Coast Guard provides ice-breaking assistance. Air transportation is regulated by the government. Air Canada, privatized in 1989, is one of the world's largest carriers.

Education: Education in Canada is under the control of the provinces. A public system of education was established as early as the 1840s and 1850s. Education is compulsory from the age of 6 or 7, and 15 or 16 years is the minimum leaving age. Postsecondary education is mostly publicly financed by the provinces and is continually expanding. An excellent system exists with academic and work-related courses. The universities of Toronto and McGill (Montreal) are known throughout the world, and all provinces support universities through public funding. In 1990-92, over 553,931 students were enrolled in universities and colleges, and 24,000 persons were enrolled part-time.

Principal Products:
Agriculture: Apples, grapes, peaches, barley, flaxseed, hay, oats, rye, soybeans, wheat, carrots, corn, potatoes, sugar beets, tomatoes, cattle, chickens, hogs, sheep and lambs, turkeys, dairy products, honey, maple products
Fishing: Cod, crab, flounder, sole, haddock, halibut, herring, lobster, mackeral, perch, redfish, salmon, scallops, tuna, whitefish
Forestry: Logs and pulpwood (for paper)
Mining: Antimony, asbestos, cadmium, coal, copper, gold, gypsum, iron ore, lead, natural gas, molybdenum, nickel, petroleum, potash, rock salt, silver, sulphur, titanium, uranium, zinc
Furs: Beaver, fisher, lynx, marten, mink, muskrat, seal. Canada is recognized as the producer of the finest wild furs in the world.
Manufacturing: Chemicals, electrical products, food and beverages, machinery, metal products, paper and related products, transportation equipment, wood products

IMPORTANT DATES

c. 1003-15–Vikings settle at L'Anse aux Meadows, on the northern tip of Newfoundland, for three years

1497–John Cabot lands on the East Coast of Canada

1534–Jacques Cartier sails into the Gulf of St. Lawrence

1576–Martin Frobisher searches for the Northwest Passage

1585-87–John Davis searches for the Northwest Passage

1605–Sieur de Monts settles at Port Royal (in what is now Nova Scotia)

1608–Samuel de Champlain chooses Quebec as site for settlement

1610–Henry Hudson discovers Hudson Bay

1642–Ville Marie (Montreal) is founded

1670–The Hudson's Bay Company is founded

1682–LaSalle reaches the mouth of the Mississippi River

1749–Halifax is founded by Edward Cornwallis

1750-53–2,500 foreign Protestants arrive in Nova Scotia

1759–British defeat French at Quebec on the Plains of Abraham

1760-77–8,000 pro-Loyalist New England planters arrive in Canada

1763–The Treaty of Paris surrenders most of New France to England

1774–The Quebec Act gives French Canadians language, legal, and religious rights

1775–The American Revolution begins; Americans occupy Montreal but are repulsed at Quebec City

1784–The colony of New Brunswick is established

1785–The first university, Kings College (later the University of New Brunswick), is established

1791–Constitutional Act divides Quebec into Upper and Lower Canada and grants each a legislative assembly

1793–Alexander Mackenzie crosses British Columbia to the coast

1808–Simon Fraser reaches the mouth of the Fraser River from the east

1812–First settlers led by Thomas Douglas, earl of Selkirk, arrive at Red River, near Winnipeg

1812-14–U.S. declares war on Britain; attempts to invade Canada are repulsed

1818–49th parallel accepted as the boundary between U.S. and Canada for the area between Lake of the Woods and the Rocky Mountains

1836–First railway line joins La Prairie and St. Jean sur le Richelieu

1838–Rebellions in Lower Canada dn Upper Canada

1840–Act of Union joins Upper Canada and Lower Canada into Province of Canada

1846–Western boundary between the United States and Canada is extended from the Rockies to the Pacific Coast

1848–Responsible government established in Nova Scotia, and Province of Canada

1858–Gold rush to the Fraser

1867–The Province of Canada (Quebec and Ontario), Nova Scotia, and New Brunswick join in a confederation to form the Dominion of Canada

1869 – Red River uprising; Northwest Territories purchased from Hudson's Bay Company

1870 – Province of Manitoba joins the Dominion

1871 – British Columbia joins the Dominion

1873 – Prince Edward Island joins the Dominion

1880 – Canada acquires Britain's claim to the Arctic

1885 – East and West coasts linked by Canadian Pacific Railway; Northwest Rebellion led by Louis Riel results in the creation of the state of Manitoba

1896 – Gold is discovered in the Klondike

1905 – Alberta and Saskatchewan become provinces

1914-18 – Canada sends 500,000 troops to Europe in World War I

1929 – Great Depression

1931 – Statute of Westminster; Canada achieves complete independence from Britain

1939-40 – World War II

1949 – Newfoundland joins the Dominion and becomes the tenth province

1954-59 – The St. Lawrence Seaway makes the Great Lakes accessible to seagoing vessels – a joint effort of Canada and the United States

1962 – Trans-Canada Highway opens

1965 – New flag adopted

1980 – Quebec holds referendum and votes to remain in the Confederation

1982 – Constitution Act passed

1985 – Canada and the United States dispute ownership rights in the Arctic waters of the Northwest Passage

1988 – Canada and the United States sign a bold trade pact removing tariffs and other trade restrictions between the two countries, creating the world's largest open market

1991 – Some of the worst forest fires in Quebec history force evacuation of communities on the north shore of the St. Lawrence

1992 – The Toronto Blue Jays win Major League Baseball's 89th World Series over the Atlanta Braves in the first win ever for a team outside the U.S.

1993 – The ruling Progressive Conservative Party chooses Defense Minister Kim Campbell as its leader, making her the first woman prime minister in Canada's history; Canada is the first nation to ratify the North American Free Trade Agreement between Canada, Mexico, and the United States; in October Campbell is replaced by Jean Chrétien of the Liberal Party

1994 – The NAFTA treaty takes effect as unemployment and inflation increase; public opinion poles indicate that 70 percent of the population is opposed to the treaty and blame it for economic problems

1995 – A referendum regarding Quebec's break-up with Canada is defeated on October 30 in favor of staying with Canada by a slim margin of 50.6 percent

IMPORTANT PEOPLE

William Aberhart (1878-1943), spellbinding orator; premier of Alberta (1935-43)

Margaret Atwood (1939-   ), poet and novelist, author *Life Before Man*

Robert Baldwin (1804-58), politician who helped obtain responsible government for the Province of Canada

Harold Ballard (1903-1990), majority owner of Toronto Maple Leafs

Frederick G. Banting (1891-1941), discoverer of insulin with J.J.R. Macleod, C.H. Best, and J.B. Collip

Pierre Berton (1920-   ), author of *The National Dream* and *The Last Spike*

Gerard Bessette, novelist, author of *Les Anthropiodes*

Charles H. Best (1899-1978), codiscoverer of insulin

Marguerite Bourgeous (1628-1708), founder of religious order, canonized in 1982

Joseph Brant (1742-1807), and Molly Brant (c. 1736-96), Mohawk Loyalists who helped their people settle in the Grand Valley, Ontario

Jean de Brebeuf (1593-1649), Jesuit missionary, martyr, killed in Huronia

Samuel Bronfman (1931-   ), industrialist, chairman of Seagram Company and the Montreal Expos

John By (1781-1836), English engineer who designed and built the Rideau Canal

Emily Carr (1871-1945), painter, best known for sketches of West Coast Indian life and landscapes

George Etienne Cartier (1814-73), leading French-Canadian father of confederation

Samuel de Champlain (c. 1570-1635), mapmaker, explorer, often called "Father of New France"

Sir Samuel Cunard (1787-1865), shipowner and founder of Cunard Line

Robertson Davies (1913-   ), writer, author of the Deptford Trilogy (*Fifth Business*, *The Manticore*, and *World of Wonders*)

Dekanahwideh, founder of the Five Nations Confederacy (Mohawk, Oneida, Cayuga, Seneca, and Onondaga) and culture of the Iroquois

Sir James Douglas (1803-77), governor of British Columbia, often called "Father of British Columbia"

Maureen Forrester (1930-   ), contralto

Simon Fraser (1776-1862), explorer and the first white man to follow the Fraser River to its mouth

Glenn Gould (1932-82), classical pianist and composer

Group of Seven (Franklin Carmichael, 1890-1945; Lawren Harris, 1885-1970; A.Y. Jackson, 1882-1974; Franz Johnston, 1888-1949; Arthur Lismer, 1885-1969; J.E.H. Macdonald, 1873-1932; and F.H. Varley, 1881-1969), a group of artists who (together with Tom Thomson, 1877-1917, who died before the group was formed), established the first school of impressionist painting in Canada

Thomas Chandler Haliburton (1796-1865), jurist and humorist, creator of newspaper character Sam Slick in *The Clockmaker, or The Sayings and Doings of Sam Slick of Slickville*

Samuel Hearne (1745-92), explorer, who with the Chipewyan chief, Matonabee, explored the Northwest Territories as far west as the Coopermine River and north to the Arctic Ocean

Anne Hebert (1916-   ), writer of *Kamouraska* and *Les Fous des Basson*

Ramon Hnatyshyn, appointed governor-general in 1990

Joseph Howe (1804-73), politician, orator, and writer; established freedom of press; at first fought entry of Nova Scotia into Canadian Dominion, but later accepted post in federal cabinet; fought for responsible government

Mel Hurtig (1912-   ), publisher, author, and proponent of Canadian nationalism

Pauline Johnson (1861-1913), poet who celebrated the heritage of the Indians; daughter of a Mohawk chief

Karen Kain (1951-   ), principal dancer of the National Ballet of Canada

Paul Kane (1810-71), author and painter of Native peoples; wrote *Wanderings of an Artist among the Indians of North America*

Yousuf Karsh (1908-   ), portrait photographer

Henry Kelsey (c. 1667-1724), explorer who journeyed to the prairies in 1690-92 from Hudson Bay

Kenojuak Asevak (1927-   ), Inuit artist

Rene-Robert LaSalle (1643-87), explorer; the first European to sail down the Mississippi; his trip was the basis for French claims to the Louisiana Territory

Margaret Laurence (1926-87), writer, author of *The Diviners*

Pierre La Verendrye (1685-1749), explorer who opened area from Lake Superior to Missouri for French fur traders

Rene Lavesque (1922-87), leader of Quebec separatist movement, Quebec premier (1976-85)

Stephen Leacock (1869-1944), economist, humorist, and author of *Sunshine Sketches of a Little Town*

Roger Lemelin (1919-   ), writer, author of *Les Plouffe*

John A. Macdonald (1815-91), chief architect of the Confederation and Canada's first prime minister

Sir Alexander Mackenzie (1764-1820), explorer and first European to cross North America overland

William Lyon Mackenzie (1795-1861), leader of rebellion of 1837 in Upper Canada

Hugh MacLennan (1907-90), novelist, author of *Two Solitudes*

Marshall McLuhan (1911-80), writer and thinker, best known for his work on communication—*The Medium Is the Massage*

Sir Ernest MacMillan (1893-1973), composer, conductor, and musician

Paul Maisonneuve (1612-76), founder and first governor of Montreal

Vincent Massey (1887-1967), diplomat, patron of the arts, and first Canadian-born governor-general

John Molson (1763-1836), entrepreneur, founded a brewing company that became one of the largest corporations in Canada

Lucy Maud Montgomery (1874-1942), author of *Anne of Green Gables* and seven sequels

Raymond Moriyama (1929-   ), architect; some of his works are the Ontario Science Centre and the Scarborough City Centre, Ontario

Norval Morrisseau, Native artist

Farley Mowat (1921-   ), author of books on nature and Canadian Arctic territory

Daphne Odjig, Native artist

William Osler (1849-1919), physician and author of astronomical and theological works

Louis Joseph Papineau (1786-1871), led movement for reform in Lower Canada

Lester B. Pearson (1897-1972), prime minister (1963-68), winner of Nobel Peace Prize for organizing United Nations intervention in Suez Canal crisis in 1957

Pitseolak Ashoona (1907-83), artist

Pierre Radisson (1636-1710), explorer, fur trader, helped found the Hudson's Bay Company

John Richardson (1796-1852), novelist, author of *Wacousta*

Louis Riel (1844-85), Metis leader whose execution for treason is still a subject of controversy

Mordecai Richler (1931-   ), novelist, author of *The Apprenticeship of Duddy Kravitz*

Gabrielle Roy (1909-83), novelist, author of *Le Libraire*

Hans Selve (1907-82), discovered evidence that mental stress affects bodily functions

Robert W. Service (1874-1958), poet, wrote *Songs of a Sourdough*; known as ''Poet of the Yukon''

Yves Theriault (1915-   ), novelist, author of *Agaguk* and *Ashini*

Michel Tremblay, playwright, author of *Les Belles-Soeurs*

George Vancouver (1757-98), explorer and mapmaker who charted the West Coast. Vancouver Island and the city of Vancouver are named after him.

Sir William Van Horne (1843-1916), railway manager who helped organize building of the Canadian Pacific Railway

Percé Rock, Quebec

INDEX

Page numbers that appear in boldface type indicate illustrations

141

About the Author

Jenifer Shepherd was graduated from the University of London, England. She has taught history and geography, and edited and written social studies textbooks. She is married and has five children.